# A LADY'S TRUST

## ROSE ROOM ROGUES ~ BOOK TWO

### CALLIE HUTTON

## ABOUT THE BOOK

Driscoll Rose and his two brothers own and run The Rose Room, a well-known and profitable gaming club in London. Unknown to those who visit and spend their money there, the brothers also work for the Crown in positions only known to a mysterious man at the Home Office.

Miss Amelia Pence is on the run from her step-brother who has nefarious plans for her. Late one rainy night she crawls into Driscoll's office window and falls at his feet. Intrigued by the woman, he offers her a job as the only female dealer in the Rose Room.

Amelia is secretive about who she is, and where she lives since she can trust no one, much to Driscoll's frustration. The growing attraction between them and his desire for her is causing him to dismiss the fact that crowds of gamblers swarm her table each evening, but the profits she turns in are not what they should be.

*September 1891*
*London, England*

*M*r. Driscoll James Rose, second son of the late Earl of Huntington, brother to the current Earl of Huntington, and part owner of The Rose Room, the most exclusive and popular gaming club in all of London, tossed his pencil down on his desk in frustration.

*Bloody, bloody, hell.*

He removed his spectacles and rubbed his eyes with his fists. No matter how hard he tried, of late he could not keep his mind on his work.

The malaise he'd been suffering from the past few weeks was not going away. His intelligent mind knew there was no reason for it. He had no money worries, the ladies considered him handsome, he could pretty much pick and choose whatever woman he wanted, either for an evening or a lifetime, and although not a titled lord himself, he was a member of the nobility through his father and brother. So why the hell did he feel lost? Like he was floating, just getting through each day? Waiting for something to happen?

The excitement of owning, running, and making a success of a gaming club had worn off. Now it was only work. And drudgery at that.

Three years ago, he and his younger brother, Dante, had approached Hunt, the eldest of the Rose brothers with a plan to open a gaming club. Although gambling was illegal, there were several places in London that offered such entertainment. The authorities were willing to look the other way for an owner who was a member of the *ton*, as well as the recipient of an occasional evening of gratis entertainment for themselves.

The brothers had worked out a plan where Hunt would provide the initial financing of the business and would hold a small interest in the profits. Driscoll and Dante would do the bulk of the work, although Hunt would appear every so often to mix with the clients and observe that his investment was doing well.

Driscoll pushed away from his desk and slumped in his chair, his legs stretched out, his feet crossed at the ankles. Why wasn't it enough anymore? According to his younger brother, he needed to avail himself of an exclusive mistress to see to his needs. Hunt, on the other hand, who was recently wed and nauseatingly besotted with his new wife thought Driscoll should join him in the chains of matrimony.

The first seemed like too much involvement, and the second was unquestionably too much involvement. He'd heard Dante's grumbling about the demands his mistresses made. That usually happened a week or two before he gave said mistress a fine piece of jewelry along with her congé and moved onto the next one.

That was much too intricate for Driscoll. Not that he never indulged, he was a man after all with a man's needs, but the thought of providing a woman with clothing, food, housing, and expensive trinkets for the sole purpose of satisfying his sexual needs left him cold.

And doing the same for a life-long commitment of a wife left him terrified.

"It looks like we need to offer an escort home to Lord Benson again." Dante entered the office and dropped into a chair and leaned back linking his fingers at the back of his head.

"In his cups?"

"Yes. Absolutely sotted. He can barely make it from table to table. I'm afraid he might decide to bring up all that expensive brandy he's been drinking onto the gaming floor."

Driscoll stood. "I need a break from these financial records, anyway. I'll take care of it."

Dante plunked his feet on his desk and closed his eyes. "Good. I could use a break."

Driscoll made his way down the thick-carpeted stairs to the gaming floor. As expected, the room was crowded and the gaming tables full. He nodded to Stephen Welsh, the man running the Hazard game for a nice group of gamblers. As he made his way through the room, moving from table to table, he commented and joked with various members until he spotted Benson.

The man was swaying on his feet while he watched the dice play. Dante had been correct. The man appeared a bit green. Driscoll looked around and waved David Jenkins, one of the security men, over.

"Yes, Mr. Rose." The dark-haired guard stood almost as tall as Driscoll. He'd been in their employ since they opened and had the ability to handle delicate matters without causing a scene.

"We need to get Benson out of here." Driscoll nodded in the man's direction. "Use one of our older carriages in case he casts up his accounts during the ride home."

"I believe his lordship arrived in his own carriage."

Leave it to Jenkins to know everything that needed

to be known. "Perfect, then. Assist him outside and get him on his way."

The guard nodded and strode to where Benson stood. He leaned down and said something that had the man immediately straightening up. Jenkins patted him on the shoulder in a friendly but determined manner and led him from the room.

Problem solved.

Driscoll wandered the area, but the usual thrill he received from watching what he and his brother had accomplished was just not there. Maybe it was time to visit with Sir Phillip DuBois-Gifford, their contact at the Home Office to see if there was an assignment for him to add some excitement to his life.

Unbeknownst to practically everyone in London, the Rose brothers were oftentimes called upon by Sir Phillip to handle delicate matters for the Crown. Sir Phillip was not on any record of employment with the Home Office, but he managed to work behind the scenes and correct sensitive situations near and dear to the Prime Minister and sometimes the Queen herself.

After Driscoll had spent another thirty minutes meandering the rooms while consuming two brandies, he returned to the upstairs office. Dante was still in the same position, snapping a rubber band.

"All right, little brother. Break over." He shoved Dante's feet off the desk.

"Benson on his way?" Dante asked as he stood and stretched.

"Yes. Luckily the man brought his own carriage so any consequences from his overindulgence would be his own mess."

Dante left the room and Driscoll sat once again at his desk in the corner and pulled the ledger closer. He had to push himself to focus, but eventually settled down and continued his work, albeit with no more enthusiasm than when he'd left.

It was nearing midnight when a noise startled him, and he looked up. The sound seemed to come from the window on the far side of the room. He'd left it open earlier when the room seemed to grow stuffy. Perhaps it was a branch from the tree outside hitting the side of the building.

He shrugged and continued with his work. Within seconds, another thump caught his attention. He looked up to see a young man climb through the window, stumble, then fall to the floor with a crash.

\* \* \*

MISS AMELIA SMYTHE grunted as her hip hit the floor and a sharp pain shot down her leg like an arrow hitting its mark. She winced, but didn't cry out, trying to remain as silent as possible. From what she had observed perched on the tree branch from which she'd just jumped, this room was unoccupied.

She climbed to her feet and straightened her jacket.

"May I help you, sir?"

Amelia almost fell back out the window at the sound of a man's voice. She whirled around and stared for a few seconds at two deep brown, possibly angered, eyes. "Why are you here?" She barely got the words out.

The man, his dark brown hair falling over his broad forehead, was quite good-looking the female part of her noticed. He merely raised his eyebrows and continued to stare at her. Given this unexpected setback, it was probably best if she got out of there as quickly as possible. "Um, if you will excuse me, sir, I will leave now." She waved at the window.

"Wait!" He walked toward her, his full lips tipped in a slight grin. "You're not a young man."

She shook her head and sucked in a breath as the room seemed to shrink as the man grew closer. He was broad-shouldered, tall, and quite imposing. His aristocratic features blended well with his deep brown eyes. A slight tingling erupted in her middle and all the available air in the room had seemed to rush out the opened window.

She'd watched the space from outside on her perch while another man had sat with his feet up on a desk, snapping rubber bands. Eventually, he got up, stretched, and left. She hadn't seen anyone else enter.

Her mistake.

"No. I am not a young man. I'm sorry for the disturbance, sir." She nodded toward the desk she hadn't seen from the tree and said, "I will leave you to your work, then."

He reached out and grabbed her hand, a frown of curiosity on his face. "Why did you crawl through my window?"

In full panic now with the man gripping her hand, she blurted the first thing that came to mind. "It's raining outside."

Although it seemed impossible, he raised his brows even higher. "You do not possess an umbrella?"

She shook her head, wondering if she could make an escape before he called the Watch. Although truth be known, if they hauled her off to jail it would be better than what she had waiting for her at home.

No. She mis-spoke. Or rather, mis-thought. She had no home. Her horrid stepbrother, Randolph had committed the shocking offense of using her to pay a gambling debt to the ghastly Daniel Lyons. She felt the need to roll her eyes every time she thought of the man's name.

Randolph, the Viscount Newton was her thirty-year old stepbrother. With nine years between them and no common parents, they'd never been close in the fifteen years their parents had been married to each other.

When not away at school, Randolph had spent a good part of his time teasing and tormenting her.

When he grew to manhood, his form of torture turned to reminding her he was the heir and when his papa died, control over her person and dowry would pass to him. With her mother dead these past few years, and then her stepfather, the former Viscount Newton, it hadn't taken long for the snake to drag her to London and offer her services as mistress to Mr. Lyons in lieu of paying his losses in a card game.

Once Randolph had told her to prepare herself because Mr. Lyons was to arrive at their doorstep in two days to 'claim' her, she had no choice but to run. Her dilemma was being without sufficient funds, and since she'd spent most of her life in the country, she had no friends in London to turn to, either.

Of course, it would have been better had she not panicked, and instead thought carefully about her circumstances and made a plan for herself before she fled the house. At least a plan better than tumbling through the window into this man's office to escape the bad weather.

She cleared her throat, pushing her thoughts from her old dilemma to this new one. "Actually, I do possess an umbrella, but unfortunately, I do not have it with me." She tugged her hand from the man's hold and edged back toward the window, keeping her eye on him. "Now if you will excuse me. . ."

Quickly, he reached out and took her hand again. "No. I am not going to let you crawl back out the window and possibly break your neck."

She huffed. What was it with men who thought they could tell one what to do and what not to do? She was a woman grown of twenty-one years.

Adopting a pleasant demeanor, she said, "No need to concern yourself, sir. I will be fine, I can assure you." She wiped the rain from her cheeks. "I made it up here, didn't I?"

Apparently, her attempt at levity fell flat as the man

continued to stare at her. "You will tell me who you are, why you are dressed like a man, and why you climbed through my window." He nodded in the direction of the window.

She shifted from one foot to the other. Mayhap if she gave him some information, he would let her go. "I am Miss Amelia Pence." There was no point in offering her correct name. The last thing she needed was him tracking down her stepbrother. "It is quite wet out there and I saw the light in your window and hoped to spend only a short time attempting to dry off and warm up." As if to validate her words, she shivered, then raised her chin.

There. She had given him an almost-honest answer.

"Did it not occur to you to enter through the front door to do the same?" She hated how he seemed to switch from anger to laughing at her. "And why the outfit?" He flicked his finger up and down.

He was becoming quite vexing. Amelia drew herself up, attempting to look impressive even though she was in trousers, soaking wet and just made a complete cake of herself by falling through the window. "Why I am wearing these clothes is none of your concern, sir. Now if you will excuse me and seeing that you won't let me go back out the way I entered, I will just use that door behind you to make my way downstairs and exit the building."

Feeling less confident than her words, she moved to go around him and came to a complete halt when he stepped in front of the door. "No." He shook his head, again with a bit of levity in his look. "I am afraid I demand more answers from you before I let you go."

Amelia groaned and shivered again. This solution to escape Randolph was becoming more vexing than her problem.

---

## 2

*D*riscoll doubted the woman had given her real name, or a reason why the devil she was climbing through the window. However, he was having more fun at her expense then he'd had in ages.

She was a pretty little thing. Big blue eyes and blonde ringlets, now wet and plastered to her forehead. Plump lips perfect for kissing tempted him and a small nose with a scattering of light freckles across her cheeks gave her an elfish look and brought a smile to his face. When she'd first fallen through the window, had he gotten a good look at her in wet trousers and her shirt clinging to her body, displaying all her wonderful curves, he would never had addressed her as 'sir'.

He brought himself up short, realizing that the gentleman in him should not be ogling her, but addressing how she shivered, and how those lovely, kissable lips were beginning to turn blue. Unusually cool September night air, combined with her wet clothing, could have the girl suffering from an ague.

"Despite your desire to flee my presence, I must insist you stay until you are dry." A slight rumbling from her middle presented another problem. "Have you eaten dinner?"

Her shaking grew worse, and she shrugged which meant to him that she had not eaten. He moved to the pot belly stove in the middle of the office and threw in another log.

Miss Pence did not move from her spot despite him walking away, which was promising. He grabbed his greatcoat from the coat rack near his desk and beckoned her to move toward the stove.

The poor girl seemed to have lost her spirit and shuffled meekly to the chair he pointed to and sat. "Remove your jacket."

Although her eyes grew wide at his command, she did as he bid before he draped the greatcoat over her shoulders. "I will send to the kitchen for tea and some food."

Miss Pence merely nodded.

"Can I trust you not to leave while I give instructions to the cook?"

"I w-w-won't l-leave." She pulled the coat flaps together and bent forward, getting closer to the stove.

Driscoll left, not at all sure if he could trust her not to vanish while he was gone. Since he knew nothing about the girl, it was questionable why he even cared. Was he truly so bored with his life that a wet, sopping woman, dressed in trousers, tumbling through the window in his office, interested him enough that he was reluctant to let her go until he learned her story?

*Sadly, yes.*

The club employed a cook who prepared food for the guests to partake of in a buffet style from around midnight until closing. It had originally begun as a courtesy, but despite the cost, it soon turned a nice profit when those who availed themselves of food remained and continued to gamble.

Driscoll headed to the table and filled a plate with

cheese, cold meats, bread, a berry tart, and two pieces of fruit.

"Hungry tonight, brother?" Dante eyed the full plate from across the table where he filled his own plate.

"Yes." For some reason he hesitated to share the information about the young lady—Miss Pence—with his brother. Most likely the chit would be gone by the time he returned, anyway.

To his surprise, and annoying delight, Miss Pence sat precisely where he'd left her. From his approach behind, her slumped shoulders and occasional shiver touched him. 'Twas obvious the girl was in trouble. Hopefully, over food and the tea he'd asked Cook to send up, she might be more forthcoming about her situation.

"I think this might help to warm you up, also." He handed her the plate of food that she took with enough enthusiasm to convince him that the poor girl must have been starving.

"Th-th-thank you." She clutched the plate with shaky hands.

"I don't want to be disrespectful, Miss Pence, but I think the best way for you to warm up is to remove your wet clothes."

He winced when her eyes widened, and it appeared as though she was about to bolt.

"No. No, that is not what I meant." He ran his fingers through his hair. "I mean there is a bedroom on this floor—"

Miss Pence jumped up, placed the plate of food on the table in front of her and made for the door, his greatcoat dropping to the floor. *Bloody hell*, he was making a muck of things.

"No. Please." He bolted ahead of her and blocked the door.

"Move away from the door, sir." She raised her chin, the wet curls clinging to her forehead. The combination of her shaky voice and body only made him feel worse. The last thing he wanted was to frighten the girl and have her race back out into the foul weather.

He moved aside. "Please allow me to explain. I went about this all wrong."

She placed her hand on the door latch but didn't open the door, the caution in her eyes making him back up.

"There is another room on this floor," he smartly did not mention the word 'bed', "where you can change into something else. Then we can spread your clothes in front of the fire and allow them to dry while you eat." He raised his hand. "I swear to you, Miss Pence, I am a gentleman, and I would never, ever take advantage of a young lady."

She drew herself up, and although she was at least a half a foot shorter than his six feet, she gave the impression of looking down at him. "You have not even introduced yourself, sir."

"I truly beg your pardon, Miss Pence. I am Mr. Driscoll Rose. I am brother to the Earl of Huntington. My other brother, Mr. Dante Rose and myself, own this club."

She visibly relaxed, but not completely. "I do not travel in Society, Mr. Rose, so I must admit I do not recognize your brother's title. However, I am familiar with The Rose Room, which is, I assume, where I managed to make my very awkward and embarrassing entrance?"

Despite her disheveled appearance and abrupt arrival, she managed to enthrall him further with her humor, and Driscoll felt more than the usual ennui for the first time in weeks. "Yes. This is the second floor of The Rose Room."

\* \* \*

AMELIA BREATHED A SIGH OF RELIEF. The Rose Room was the one place her brother would never find her. He'd been banned from the elite club for fist-fighting over three weeks before.

When she'd spotted the open, welcoming, and well-lit window at the back of the building, she had no idea what the structure housed. A large oak tree, with branches a mere few feet from the window was far too tempting not to climb.

As she studied Mr. Rose, she had no idea how to accomplish it, but if she could remain here until morning, it would give her time to come up with a plan while assuaging her hunger and staying warm and dry.

Depending on this nice man to be the gentleman he claimed, she came up with a decision. "Yes, Mr. Rose. I believe a dry set of clothes would be most welcome."

The smile he offered her caused butterflies to dance in her middle. However, she was neither at a time, nor in a place to encourage attention from a man. She was already on the run from two men. What she needed was a way to earn money without her stepbrother finding out so she could leave London.

"Excellent. I will have one of our maids accompany you to the room and help you change. The women we employ to clean and help in the kitchen live in rooms in the basement. Perhaps one of them will have a more appropriate outfit for you to wear."

"Thank you so much, Mr. Rose. You are too kind."

He stepped to the door and called to someone to send up Betsy. He then waved her toward the food. "Please, Miss Pence."

With a great deal of thankfulness, Amelia returned to the seat she'd so abruptly left and helped herself to some bread and cheese.

She tried very hard to be a lady, but she hadn't eaten all day and was quite hungry. Mr. Rose took the seat across from her, them both enjoying the heat from the stove. He didn't speak, but watched her in a way that was, remarkably, not threatening.

He hopped up at a knock at the door and admitted a gentleman carrying a teapot, followed by a young woman.

"Ah, good evening, Betsy. This is Miss Pence who is in need of a dry set of clothes. Can you accommodate her?"

The maid eyed Amelia and nodded. "Yes, Mr. Rose. I believe I have a few articles for Miss Pence to wear."

"Excellent. Please fetch them, and then you can escort our guest to the bedchamber down the corridor and help her change."

The maid dipped and left them, not raising a brow or showing any sort of surprise. Despite what she'd witnessed so far, perhaps Mr. Rose was a bit of a rake and oftentimes had women arrive at the club looking for clothing and a place to sleep.

She pushed that unwanted thought from her mind and continued with the food, particularly relishing the warmth from the tea.

"I don't wish to pry, Miss Pence, but may I ask why you were climbing a tree at," he looked over at the clock hanging on the wall, "one o'clock in the morning?" He grinned before she could answer. "And please don't tell me you endangered yourself by climbing a wet, slippery tree because you did not have an umbrella at hand."

Amelia wiped her mouth and placed the napkin next to her now empty plate. "I appreciate everything you did for me, Mr. Rose. However, despite your kindness I cannot tell you why. All I can do is assure you that I am not running from a crime, nor am I involved in anything illegal."

Mr. Rose stared at her, obviously not happy with her answer, but he did not seem to be overly concerned about it either.

"I thank you very much for the food and a chance to

dry off and warm up, but I will take up no more of your time." If he was going to continue questioning her, she needed to remove herself before she said something to her detriment. She rose and almost made it to the exit before a large hand slapped against the door, preventing her from opening it.

She leaned her head against it and sighed. She could not tell Mr. Rose that her stepbrother was looking for her. Even though she was of legal age, most people would return her to Randolph, assuming as her guardian, he knew what was best for her.

Hardly.

Behind her heat radiated from Mr. Rose's body, combined with the sound of his breathing, the air sweetened with mint. "No, Miss Pence."

He broke with all propriety and placed his hands on her shoulders and turned her to face him. "I will not allow you to wander the city in the rain. I don't know from what or from whom you are running, but a lady alone in the dark on the streets of London at this late hour is much too dangerous. I do not enjoy reading about murders and other horrendous things happening to lovely young women in my morning newspaper."

Amelia closed her eyes, fighting tears. She was frightened, penniless, worn out, cold, and in possession of no plan to avoid Randolph. Why was a stranger kinder to her and more concerned for her welfare than a relative who was supposed to be her guardian and protector?

Mr. Rose backed away, perhaps realizing the impropriety of touching her. "I insist you avail yourself of the empty bedroom where Betsy will take you. You may stay the night, and I assure you no one will bother you. In fact, there is a sturdy lock on the door that you can engage."

Although she hadn't been familiar with the Rose brothers in her short time in London, she'd learned that

The Rose Room was an elite gaming club owned and run by honest gentlemen connected to the nobility. Compared to Randolph's plans for her, which would result in her forever banished from polite society, and the life she had wished for herself, Mr. Rose's kind offer to let her stay at the club was a minor infraction.

"I will accept your offer, Mr. Rose. I am sure I am breaking some sort of rule of propriety in doing so, but since I know so few people in London there isn't much that can harm my reputation at this point."

He looked as though he wanted to ask a question, but her drawn appearance must have been enough for him to merely nod. "Very well. When Betsy returns with the clothes for you, I will have her take you to the bedchamber.

"I reiterate, please do engage the lock, which will make me feel better. We rarely have trouble in the club, but I do not wish to take any chances with your well-being and good name."

Shortly after their conversation, Betsy returned to the room with articles of clothing draped over her arm. At Mr. Rose's instructions the young maid escorted Amelia to a lovely bedchamber several doors down from the office where she and Mr. Rose had conversed.

The room was done in very masculine colors and style. No doubt the space was used for the brothers when they decided to stay overnight.

Once Betsy made sure Amelia knew where everything was and offered her the clothes, which consisted of a soft cotton nightgown and dressing gown, the maid left. Clenching the borrowed clothes in her hands, Amelia sat on the bed and stared out the window at the darkness.

She had a place for tonight, but what would tomorrow bring?

## 3

*A*round noon the next day, Driscoll looked up from the newspaper he was reading as Dante entered the brothers' dining room at the club and dropped into the chair across from him.

"Good morning big brother." He reached across the table and took a slice of toast from Driscoll's plate and smothered it with jam. "Can you tell me why when I tried to enter the bedroom down the hall, the door was locked?"

Driscoll shrugged and continued to eat.

"Your lack of response is interesting." Dante finished the stolen toast and crossed his arms over his chest, tilting the chair back on two legs. "Does the lock on the door have something to do with the full plate of food I saw you hustle upstairs last night? You, who never eats beyond ten o'clock at night?"

"Sometimes I eat beyond ten o'clock," Driscoll mumbled.

Raised eyebrows was Dante's only response. "Well, I know you don't have a woman in there." He gestured toward the bedroom down the hall.

Driscoll stiffened and frowned. "Why not? Why couldn't I have a woman in there?"

"Because you never raise your head from your ledgers long enough to notice anyone else. Let alone a female. And, even if you were to go against your nature and have a woman in there, even *you* wouldn't be sitting here eating breakfast while she lounges in bed."

Driscoll threw his napkin down alongside his plate. "I beg to differ. I do enjoy females, and might I remind you that I took Miss Bailey to the theater just last week?"

"Brother, she was my date that I foisted off on you." Dante stood and filled a plate from the sideboard. Eggs, bacon, tomatoes, sausage, toast and an orange.

"What do you want with the bedroom, anyway?" Driscoll studied him. "It's already after noon, you certainly don't plan to sleep now."

Dante sat and eyed his food. "No. I spent the night at Mrs. Bancroft's house, but I needed a clean shirt."

"Why don't you keep clothes at her house? You sleep there more than your own bed."

Dante grinned. "Ah, but we don't do much sleeping, brother." He took a sip of tea. "But you are avoiding my question. Why is the door locked?"

"I have a guest." Lord, how he wished to avoid this conversation. He wasn't yet sure what to make of Miss Pence. Frankly, he was relieved to hear that the door was still locked, since he hadn't the nerve to try it himself. That meant she hadn't escaped during the night.

There was no tree outside that room.

He'd decided if she had remained by morning that he would offer her temporary lodging, as long as he was comfortable that she wasn't, indeed, running from some criminal activity.

However, there was nothing about the woman that suggested wrongdoing. Of course, shimmying up trees in the rain to climb through the window of an unknown building did suggest some sort of misconduct. At least from what he'd known about proper young ladies; the ones he had avoided like the plague since they were all anxious to lead a man to the altar.

Dante stared at him. "Well?"

"What?"

His brother sighed. "Who is your 'guest' in the bedroom?"

Driscoll removed his spectacles and rubbed them with his handkerchief. A subtle maneuver to allow him time to gather his thoughts that was not lost on his brother. "Last night a woman fell through the window into the office." Bloody hell there must have been a better way to say that.

Dante's brows shot to his hairline. "Fell through the window? How the devil did she do that?"

"Climbed the tree outside the window," he mumbled.

Dante let out a low whistle. "And here I thought you led the most uninteresting life possible."

Driscoll frowned. "Do you want to hear the rest of the story, or just sit there and insult me?"

"Can I do both?" He grinned and shoveled more food into his mouth. He waved his fork at Driscoll. "Continue."

"Her name is Miss Pence. She is running from something, but I doubt—with as much assurance as I can muster—that she is a criminal."

"She climbs through the window of a gaming club in the middle of the night, and you don't think there is anything criminal about her? Did she drag her bag of ill-gotten goods with her, or leave them at the base of the tree to retrieve after she cleaned out our office?"

"Do you want to hear what I know?"

"Yes." Dante smirked.

"She said her name is Miss Amelia Pence. She was familiar with the club but didn't know that was where

19

she was seeking shelter from the rain." Driscoll took a sip of tea. "She was cold, wet, tired and hungry."

"And you being you, never noticed if she was attractive or not?"

Driscoll growled. "Yes, she is attractive, and yes I noticed. And no, before you ask, I did not offer to share the bed with her."

Dante shook his head. "Pity."

"She was frightened, Dante. Whatever it is she is running from can't be good."

"So, what is your plan here, big brother?"

"Frankly, I don't know." Alone in his own bed in his flat, he'd spent a good part of the time he should have been sleeping thinking that very same thing. She trusted him enough to accept his offer of a warm, dry bed.

"I don't mean to come across as unfeeling, but we can't have a strange woman staying at the club. I don't know anyone by the name of Pence, so that could be a made-up name. Despite your good-natured belief that she is not a criminal, we have no way of knowing if Scotland Yard is looking for her."

Driscoll sighed, hearing his very own thoughts spoken out loud by his brother. "I think we should see what she says this morning. For all I know, she went back out the window, and that would be the end of our problem."

"There is no tree outside the bedroom."

The sound of footsteps drew their attention. Miss Pence stood in the doorway, looking very much like a little lost lamb.

Everything protective in him reared its head. Driscoll took a deep breath, his heart speeding up. The devil take it, he was becoming ridiculous about the chit.

Both men stood. "Good morning, Miss Pence," Driscoll said.

She moved farther into the room and offered a

slight smile. "I just wanted to thank you for allowing me to stay here last night." She dipped a curtsy, which she didn't pull off very well since she was back into her trousers. Without saying another word, she turned to leave.

"Wait," Driscoll said and walked up to her, taking her hand in his. A very soft hand, one that only a lady would possess. She had never done hard work. Another clue to her identity. "You must at least eat breakfast before you go."

Miss Pence hesitated and glanced toward Dante.

"May I make known to you my brother, Mr. Dante Rose." Driscoll waved at his brother. "Dante, this is Miss Amelia Pence."

She backed up when Dante snorted.

\* \* \*

AMELIA FELT the heat rise to her face at the snicker coming from Mr. Dante Rose. She'd wrestled with herself for the past hour, wondering if she should just make her way out of the building without seeking Driscoll Rose to thank him.

Part of that time was also spent trying to figure out where she would go from here. She had to avoid her brother, as well as Mr. Lyons who would no doubt be searching for her as well.

Damn her stepbrother for making the stupid wager! It hurt to acknowledge that she was not surprised by what he'd done. Even though they had never been close, she didn't think he held her in such low regard to wager her into a life of disgrace and degradation.

Driscoll pulled out a chair. "Please, Miss Pence. I would like you to join us, have breakfast and possibly allow us to help you in whatever way we are able."

Dante Rose sat back, his arms crossed over his chest and watched her with all the warmth and consideration of a fox watching his prey. He was certainly nothing like his brother.

She walked to the sideboard and filled a plate with food while Driscoll fussed over her, showing her things she might like.

"Sit down, brother," Dante said. "The woman can fill her own plate."

Amelia sat in the chair Driscoll had pulled out for her.

"I thought you were anxious to change your shirt, Dante." Driscoll glared at his brother.

"Yes. I do need to change, but I wouldn't miss this show for the world." He grinned, but not in a friendly way, and Amelia's appetite vanished. She took a sip of her tea and tried to eat since she had no idea when her next meal would be.

"Please pay no attention to my brother, Miss Pence." Driscoll scowled in his direction. "I know it's hard to believe, but despite his glib remarks, underneath his façade he is a decent person. Most times."

Amelia wasn't so sure about that, but she tried her best to eat. Once she got started, she realized despite the meal she'd eaten the night before—in the middle of the night, actually—she was still quite hungry this morning.

Once she finished, with—thankfully—the brothers speaking about the previous night's winnings with each other and ignoring her, she pushed her plate aside and wiped her mouth. That seemed to be a signal between the brothers to begin questioning her.

"Miss Pence, I understand if you do not wish to tell us why you find yourself in the position you are in. However, if we are to offer you any assistance, we need to know at least a bit more about you." Driscoll pushed his spectacles up farther on his nose. "Please."

Amelia gathered her thoughts and realized there was scant information she could provide since her life had been unexceptional. At least until she was offered as a wager, then got up the nerve to escape her stepbrother and climb a tree.

"Why don't you start with why neither of us recognize your name?" Dante took the lead in questioning which immediately put her on edge. "We are familiar with almost all of London. Our patrons come from the nobility, the upper merchant class and the newly arrived American wealthy. Yet, Pence isn't a name we've heard before."

"I have spent most of my life in the country." She was going to tell the truth as much as she could without them learning who her brother was. Her governess from years ago had been adamant that it was far easier to keep one's story straight if it did not contain lies.

Driscoll nodded, seeming pleased that she at least answered one of their questions. "What brought you to London? Did you come for the purpose of joining Society and making your come-out?"

Amelia tried very hard not to laugh. A come-out? Should she tell these nice men her only come-out would be a forced introduction into the demimonde?

"No." She could not tell them she'd been ordered by her stepbrother to vacate the lovely family home in the country that she'd lived in most of her life because he'd rented it out from under her. Had she known at the time about his evil plans for her, she would have attempted to secure a position as a companion or a governess. Even working in a shop would be preferable to what her future currently looked like.

"I don't suppose you wish to tell us where you are currently living in London?" Driscoll leaned forward, resting his forearms on his thighs. He was so very nice and comfortable. Just speaking to him made her feel as though nothing bad would happen to her.

Then she realized she was dreaming, and this man was in no way responsible for her well-being. For all she knew he had a wife and several children for whom he was currently caring.

She found that to be a depressing thought.

Besides, she'd stopped believing in fairy tales when she was a child. There was no knight in shining armor going to ride up to The Rose Room and sweep her away on his white horse to live happily ever after in his castle.

She shook her head. "No. I'm afraid I cannot."

The brothers looked at each other, Dante Rose with raised brows and Driscoll with what only could be described as sympathy.

Unfortunately, that was her undoing. All the pent-up anger and fear she'd lived with since she had snuck out of her stepbrother's house rose to the surface and decided to make its presence known in a torrent of tears.

"Aw, shite," Dante said.

## 4

*D*riscoll looked frantically at his brother when Miss Pence covered her eyes and began to cry. Hell, wail was more like it.

"What should we do?" he asked Dante.

Dante shrugged. "Nothing. Let her cry it out. With your lack of knowledge and skill with the ladies, you haven't learned that these fits come on once in a while. Mostly when they want something, and you've said 'no.'"

"That seems a rather cruel assessment."

"But true. If you're disposed to do so, you can put your arm around her shoulders and pat her back a few times."

"And that seems rather personal."

Dante rolled his eyes. "Then hand her a handkerchief. Women never seem to have one on them when these fits come on."

"I'd hardly call it a fit. I think she is very distressed."

Dante nodded in her direction. "Clearly."

Miss Pence lowered her hands and glared at them. "I am right here, you know. I can hear everything you're saying." She wiped her cheeks and accepted the handkerchief Driscoll handed her.

She used it to blow her nose. "I will wash this and return it."

Driscoll waved his hand in dismissal. "No matter. I have dozens of them."

She took a deep breath. "I apologize for my unacceptable behavior."

Driscoll leaned over and patted her hand. "That is all right. No need to apologize." He glanced at Dante, who was obviously enjoying the show. Sometimes he felt the need to plant a facer on his brother.

Now was one of those times.

"If you have nowhere to go, we can. . ." Driscoll glanced sideways at Dante. "Offer you a job."

"What?" Dante almost shouted. Miss Pence began to cry again. Driscoll threw up his hands and wished himself in his office going over his books. That was safe for him. Dealing with people, especially women in distress, was definitely not his forte.

Dante might mock him about his lack of female company, but he preferred to be discreet and discriminating. No, he did not employ a mistress, the idea did not appeal, but he had enough encounters with women anxious to share the bed of one of the notorious Rose brothers to satisfy his needs, but never felt it was necessary to boast about it.

He glared at his brother. "I said we can offer Miss Pence a job." He waved in her direction. "She obviously has nowhere to go."

"We know nothing about her!"

"How much do we know about others we employ? The maids, the counters?"

"And what do you propose to have the chit do?"

A sharp intake of breath had both brothers looking at Miss Pence.

"I have not lost my hearing since the last time the two of you spoke as though I wasn't present." She stood, straightened her shoulders, and pushed in her chair. "I believe I will leave you now." She turned to Driscoll. "Thank you for the warm," she glared at Dante, "and empty bed and food. I do appreciate it."

Then she drew herself up, her cool assessment—despite her puffy red eyes—proving to Driscoll that this woman was a lady. Despite wearing trousers and climbing trees, she had been raised with all the accoutrements of nobility. "For your information, Mr. Rose, I am not a 'chit.'"

Before she made it through the doorway, Driscoll jumped from his seat and blocked the exit. If she were in trouble, he could not abandon her.

"Again, Mr. Rose?" Her smile was more a smirk than not.

"I apologize for my brother. I have the right to hire and fire people, as does Dante and my other brother, Hunt. Therefore, I am offering you a job at The Rose Room."

Dante leaned back in his chair again, grinning. "In what capacity, big brother?"

"To be determined." Driscoll walked Miss Pence back to the chair she had just abandoned. "Please. Have a seat. I will send for hot tea and we can figure this out."

Once Miss Pence was seated, Dante slapped his thighs and stood. "I still need to change my shirt and start supervising the opening of the club." He whacked Driscoll on his shoulder. "I leave you to straighten this all out." With a slight wink in Miss Pence's direction, he said, "Welcome to The Rose Room, Miss Pence."

Miss Pence's eyes followed Dante from the room, her jaw slack. She shook her head. "Your brother is a very strange man, Mr. Rose. I got the distinct impression that he had no use for me and was about to toss me out the door."

Driscoll continued to stare at the door that Dante had just exited. "Yes. He is a tad on the different side."

He then took a seat across from her just as one of

the maids brought in a fresh pot of tea. "Miss Pence, please help yourself to tea and we will discuss the situation."

She poured for herself and although he was not in need of any more tea, he accepted a cup from her.

Driscoll laid his cup in the saucer and leaned his elbows on the table. "We need to find a position for you that is suitable." He was convinced she was a lady, and he could not give her a job as a maid. The idea of having her serve drinks crossed his mind, but only briefly. Thinking of her walking around the gaming floor with some of the lecherous patrons they were known to have didn't sit well with him at all.

He would never allow anyone to touch her in his presence.

"Are you familiar with the game vingt-et-un?"

She thought for a minute. "That is a card game, correct?"

"Yes. Do you know how to play it?" If he could give her a job dealing at the vingt-et-un table it would keep her away from roaming hands, and he could keep an eye on her.

"I have played it a bit, but I wouldn't say I was good at it."

Driscoll leaned forward, excitement building when he remembered Marcus Sedgewick, one of the current vingt-et-un dealers had expressed a wish to leave that position and take up a security guard opening that was coming up when John Marshall took his pension in a few weeks.

\* \* \*

AMELIA STUDIED Driscoll as his face lit up.

"Are you willing to learn? It's not hard and the game doesn't require a lot of knowledge or skill. You merely deal the cards to yourself and those sitting at the table.

If you are somewhat familiar with it, you know the idea is to get as close as you can to twenty-one with your cards, but not go over it."

She nodded. "Yes, that much I know. But don't you want dealers who can win for you?"

"The house—which is what we call ourselves, the owners—has a built-in edge. Also, many players do not know when to quit which helps us. Also, our tables do not allow a player to double after splitting. Those house advantages make play more profitable for us."

"Oh, that is interesting." She couldn't believe she was sitting here discussing a job at a gaming club. If her poor deceased mother could see her now, she would be horrified. However, when one considered what her alternative was right now—mistress to Mr. Lyons—this was immensely preferable.

"Yes, I could do that. I would need some practice, though." Relief flooded her when she realized this man might be her knight in shining armor after all.

He reached out and covered her hand with his. "I know you are running from something—" She started to pull her hand back. "No. Just hear me out. I won't insist you tell me, but I need to know a few things."

She gave him a brief nod, wondering if all her joy was to come to an end.

"I assume since you climbed through my window that you have no place to stay?"

She offered a curt nod.

"I would be willing to allow you to stay in the bedroom you slept in last night until you receive your wages and are able to secure a room in a woman's boarding house."

"That would be wonderful."

"You may take your meals here, even after you move out—all our employees do. I can also advance you a small sum to buy a dress and whatever else you need, since we can't have you dealing cards in trousers." His smile changed his entire face. She thought him pleasant looking until he smiled, then Driscoll Rose was one of the most handsome men she'd ever seen.

She immediately chastised herself. The last thing she needed with the mess she was facing was an attraction to a man. Her initial plan to make enough money to move somewhere her stepbrother couldn't find her hadn't changed. Even though Randolph had been banned from this club, there was always the chance he could be allowed back. As much as she'd like to ask Mr. Rose to not permit that, she couldn't without telling him her story and then risking him notifying her stepbrother. At present she considered her new employer a nice man, but there was no reason to trust him just yet.

He studied her for a minute and seemed to fidget in his chair. "One more thing."

Her spirits took a downward plunge. She licked her dry lips. Here it comes, the one thing that will make her walk away. "What is that, Mr. Rose?"

"I would feel much more comfortable if you wore a mask when you worked. We can find you something that one would wear to a masquerade ball."

Amelia was stunned and her descending spirits rose again. "I think that is an excellent idea." In the off chance that one of Randolph's cronies was a member of the club, she needn't worry about being recognized.

Not that she'd spent any time with Randolph and his friends, but she did see some of them when they came to the house.

Driscoll continued. "It appears you have no belongings, so I suggest you take care of that issue today. This afternoon, I will send one of the maids with you to the store—" He stopped when she began to shake her head furiously.

She could not go to stores. "I don't wish to be more of a burden than I already am, but perhaps I can just borrow a dress from one of the female employees?"

The way he sat back and continued to stare at her with those deep brown eyes had her now squirming in her chair. It was almost as if he could see inside her, see her trepidation, feel her anxiety.

His next words proved he allowed, if not fully understood, her reluctance. "I will have you get together with Margie, another of our maids. You will instruct her on your needs, and she will purchase them. I will give you the receipts which we will deduct from your wages over the next few weeks."

She blew out the breath she'd been holding, just waiting for Mr. Rose to rescind his offer of employment and send her on her way.

There was no way she could stop the tears that gathered in her eyes, the relief was that great. She would not cry again in front of this man. She surreptitiously blotted the corners of her eyes, but the movement was not lost on him who offered her a soft smile. "Everything will be all right, Miss Pence."

She nodded, not too sure if her voice would hold if she tried to speak. After swallowing the lump in her throat a few times, she said, "Thank you so very much."

He stood and offered her his hand as if she were a true lady in a ballroom. She accepted it and stood, the warmth from his hand doing strange things to her insides. However, that she could not allow.

Not now. Not ever.

## 5

*D*riscoll searched the building for about fifteen minutes before he found his brother leaning against the doorway to the storage room, flirting with the very maid Driscoll was looking for. "Dante, the game room is not going to ready itself."

Dante winked at Margie who blushed furiously. She glanced sideways at Driscoll and dipped slightly. "Good afternoon, Mr. Rose."

His brother leaned down and spoke close to Margie's ear. "Don't let my brother frighten you. He never did learn how to deal with the ladies, and I fear he's a bit jealous."

Ignoring him, Driscoll said, "Margie, I need you to run an errand for me."

Dante sauntered off leaving the poor maid flustered. He really should not encourage them this way. Dante employed a mistress and had no intention of taking a wife, so flirting and teasing with the maids was cruel. But then as Dante pointed out, Driscoll did not exactly have an abundance of women looking to flirt with him.

That thought brought to mind the lovely young lady he just left who he'd agreed to help even though he had no reason to trust her. But then again, he had no reason not to trust her. She could have stolen what she wanted from the room she slept in the night before and made off in the morning with whatever she wanted before anyone had awakened.

"How can I help you?" Margie said after she'd recovered from Dante's blasted flirting.

"Remember the young lady Betsy brought clothes to last evening?"

"Yes. She said she was a guest of yours." Again, the blush.

Driscoll hurried on. "Yes, she was a guest, but not that kind. . ." He was afraid his face was as red as Margie's. He coughed to cover his unease and continued. "The young lady, Miss Pence, had to leave her home unexpectedly. I have just hired her, and she needs a few items of clothing to be able to work."

The devil take it, he was blushing again. This was ridiculous. Margie was his employee, and he had no reason to be uncomfortable. Let her think what she wanted.

"You will find her upstairs in the bedroom. She will give you a list of things she needs." He reached into his pocket and withdrew some bills and handed them to her. "This should cover what you will purchase. Be sure to bring me the receipts since I will be deducting the cost from her wages."

Margie's eyes grew wide as she accepted the money. There. That should stop any gossip.

"Is Miss Pence to be another maid?"

He shook his head. "No, she will be working on the gaming floor."

More raised eyebrows. "A woman, sir?"

"Yes. Now go on up and get the list and hurry along."

He took a deep breath as Margie hurried off. Now he could return to his work and go over the last evening's receipts. He preferred that to dealing with uncomfortable requests of maids and thoughts of Miss Pence sliding trousers down her shapely legs and changing into lady's undergarments.

Bloody hell. What was wrong with him?

ABOUT FOUR HOURS later he was fully engrossed in his work and had managed to put Miss Pence and her clothing issues far from his mind. He felt better, more in balance with his usual self.

A soft knock on the office door drew his attention. The door opened and Miss Pence stuck her head in. "Do you have a free minute?"

"Certainly." He waved her in. And immediately lost his breath. She had gone from a trouser-clad, sopping wet mess to a beautiful young lady with all the grace and polish one sees on a ballroom floor in London.

She wore a deep blue satin dress with the front drawn across her middle to gather in the back. The neckline exposed enough of her bosom to entice but was not at all improper. The sleeves were wide at her upper arms, but snug fitting from the elbows down.

His eyes roamed to her hands, soft and graceful, joined together and resting against her stomach. Her hair had been brushed to a golden delight, then pulled back into a chignon with spirals of curls hugging her forehead and temples.

She was magnificent.

And every man who came to the club would see her. And talk to her. And flirt with her. Maybe he should have hired her as a maid after all. One who would remain in the background.

Then he brought himself up short. Miss Pence was an employee. Only that. Plus, he knew nothing of her background and hadn't yet decided if he even trusted her.

"You look lovely, Miss Pence." He barely got the

words out, feeling like a youth faced with his first sweetheart.

She offered a slight dip and blushed charmingly. "Thank you."

"I see that Margie was able to find something that suits you."

"Yes. She was very helpful. Thank you for that, too."

He waved her to the chair in front of his desk. "How can I help you?"

"I wondered when I would actually begin my employment. I certainly need some practice with the game before I attempt to act as a dealer."

Driscoll tapped his pencil on the desk. "Yes, you do indeed. However, we do not allow ladies on the game floor."

The rule that had applied since they opened the door was men were permitted to bring their mistresses with them. A few women from the demimonde visited occasionally, but ladies were not allowed. The brothers felt it was not a proper place for ladies. Although, it was obvious to him that they had just employed a lady to not only appear on the gaming floor, but actually work as a dealer.

The idea of Miss Pence wearing a mask had been a stroke of genius. Whatever issue she was dealing with, along with her reputation, would not be worsened by her job at The Rose Room.

* * *

"THEN HOW WILL I learn what I need to know?" Amelia tried her best to calm her racing heart, which seemed to happen whenever she was around Driscoll.

She smoothed out the gown Margie had purchased for her to distract herself. She'd been quite pleased when the maid had returned with the articles of clothing she had requested. The gown was lovely and fit perfectly. Thank heaven for ready-made clothes. The maid had even been clever enough to also purchase a brush, comb, toothbrush and tooth powder, along with a night rail and dressing gown. All items she'd not thought about in her race from the house.

Amelia felt as though she'd been traveling in a whirlwind. She had gone through so much in the past couple of days it was a wonder she was able to think straight. Now she faced the challenge of employment. She'd never worked a day in her life, and if things had gone the way her mother and stepfather had planned, she would have had her come-out in London and married off to a gentleman who would take care of her for the rest of her life.

Alas, now she was left in the care of despicable Randolph. Although she had never understood the animosity between him and his father, she now believed her stepfather was very much aware of the son's nefarious ways. 'Twas too bad he hadn't made the necessary changes in his will so Randolph would not end up controlling her and her dowry, which she was quite certain no longer existed.

But she'd never been the sort of person who wailed at life's problems. Which was why she now found herself sitting in a gaming club about to take a job as a card dealer, thwarting Randolph's intention to make her a man's mistress.

"I think the best way to make you comfortable with vingt-et-un is to play several hands. First as a player, and then as a dealer."

"That sounds like a perfect idea, but who will play with me?"

Driscoll cleared his throat and ran his finger around the inside of his stiff collar, looking a bit uncomfortable as if she had said something inappropriate. "I will find a few employees to help you, but unfortunately the club opens in a short while, so I suggest you have something to eat, and we will work on your training tomorrow."

Her shoulders slumped. "What will I do for the rest of the night?" She'd already spent the day wandering the bedroom, with nothing to do and nothing to read. In desperation she had taken a nap. That little bit of sleep left her energized, so she really needed something to keep herself busy for the rest of the evening.

"Are you good with numbers?" Driscoll asked.

"Yes." Maths had been her best subject growing up. She'd had an excellent governess who believed young ladies had a brain similar to men and could certainly learn maths and science.

"Then perhaps you can help me. We are nearing the end of the month as well as the quarter, so I need to pull a lot of numbers from various ledgers and combine them into another ledger."

"I would love to do that." Lord, anything except return to the bedroom and stare at the walls.

He frowned. "It can be tedious."

She shook her head. "That's fine. I've worked on my stepfather's books, so I know how much. . ." She stopped, realizing what she'd said. Driscoll Rose, not being a stupid man picked up right away on what she was saying. She could see the light in his eyes. "Go on."

She shrugged. "Nothing. It's just that I know I can be a help to you."

He grinned and her heart did that double thump again. He pulled out a gold timepiece from the pocket of his waistcoat and checked the time. "Why don't I escort you to the dining room and we'll have some dinner? Then I can show you what you can do to help."

Still attempting to recover from her *faux pas*, she stood and shook out her skirts. "Yes, I would like that."

There was something about Driscoll Rose that loosened her tongue. He was so easy to talk to, and she had a horrid feeling if they spent much time together she would blurt out her disgrace. Until she could trust him not to turn her over to her stepbrother, she would watch her words carefully.

As they made their way down the corridor from the office, Amelia asked, "Do all the staff eat in the dining room?"

Driscoll placed his hand on her lower back to direct her through the doorway to the dining room. She immediately felt flushed, warmth emanating from where his hand rested on her body. He didn't seem to make much of it, and she was sure he was merely being a gentleman. No need to make anything of it.

"No. The maids, security guards and other employees eat in the kitchen in the basement. That is also where those who live here have their rooms."

Dante rose from his seat when they entered the room.

She slipped into the seat Driscoll held out for her. "Then why am I not eating and sleeping downstairs, also?"

Dante smirked across the table from where she was seated. "Despite what you want us to believe, Miss Pence, we are aware of your station in life. You are not of the maid and 'employee' ilk."

She raised her chin. This man was nothing like his brother. He seemed to be able to antagonize her every time he opened his mouth. "And how do you know that, Mr. Rose?"

"Dante, if you please, since we are both Mr. Rose and I don't want you to mix us up. However informal we are in the club, though, we do revert to 'Mister' and now 'Miss' on the game room floor." He motioned to the maid standing near the sideboard to serve.

In answer to her question, he added, "'Tis quite obvious that everything about you tells us you are a lady, born and bred. The way you hold yourself, your gait, your manners, your way of speaking."

She thought about that while the maid began to serve them a fine dinner of baked whitefish in a wine sauce, slices of beef, roasted carrots and turnips, and boiled potatoes with pieces of leek.

A man dressed in formal attire poured them wine. Although her time in London had never been spent at fancy *ton* events, there was no doubt that the Rose brothers had been also born and bred as gentlemen. This array of food would most likely be served at any *ton* dinner party.

"Here's to our new employee," Dante said as he raised his glass.

She glanced sideways at Driscoll who lifted his glass slightly. "Welcome to The Rose Room."

## 6

*D*riscoll was still reeling from how Miss Pence had affected him when she'd walked into his office in that gown. After he made the offer to her for a position as a dealer, he'd sought out his brother and they both agreed that she was not from the working class. As a dealer, while seeming to be even more notorious than her working as a maid, she would retain her dignity while the mask would protect her reputation.

As the meal continued and the three spoke of various innocuous subjects, he was beginning to regret his offer to have her help him with the books. The two of them alone together in the office for hours while they did the tedious work might be too much for him to handle.

Her scent, her soft laugh at something Dante just said, and her very presence would be a distraction he did not need. On the other hand, his curiosity about the woman, where she came from, who she actually was, and why she had no home despite being of the upper crust, teased his brain, making him want to learn the answers.

"Do you ride, Miss Pence?" Dante asked.

"I do. But it has been a while."

She tilted her head slightly and directed her question to Dante. "Since Driscoll told me to address you as 'Dante' why do you continue to call me 'Miss Pence'?"

Driscoll smiled at her. "We prefer to keep things formal among our employees while on the game floor. I am referred to as Mr. Rose as is my brother. Since I am not on the game floor very much, there isn't a great deal of confusion between us."

"Then you must call me Amelia when not working." She put her fork down and studied him. "If I am to be an employee, I expect to be treated as the others." She waved her hand around. "I am the only employee eating here, I am the only employee with a bedroom on this floor."

Driscoll looked over at Dante who took a sip of wine and shrugged. "Your call, big brother."

He did not want to relegate Amelia to the basement with the other employees. He attempted to convince himself it was merely because she was a lady, and not that he thought of her as someone special.

He cleared his throat and looked over at her. "I believe for now we will leave the sleeping and eating arrangements as they are. We will continue to address you as Miss Pence while you are working on the floor." He gestured to the footman to pour them all more wine.

David Jenkins, the security guard the brothers depended on to keep patrons from fisticuffs when things didn't go their way, entered the dining room. He gave a slight bow and turned to Dante. "I apologize for interrupting your dinner, but there is a problem with the Hazard table. When you are through with your meal, can you see to it?"

Dante finished the dregs of his wine glass, wiped his mouth and stood. "I am finished." He nodded at Driscoll and Amelia and left the room.

"We generally have tea and dessert. Would you care

41

for some?" Driscoll felt the strain of Dante's absence immediately. He and Amelia were alone again. Which is what they would be for the rest of the night. He needed to put her from his mind. Perhaps he should not be treating her differently.

She placed her elbow on the table and rested her chin on her upraised hand. "I am too full for dessert, but I would love some tea."

The maid immediately left the room to fetch the tea. The silence was deafening. It annoyed him that Dante's departure had put him on edge.

During the dinner, he'd spent time studying Amelia's hand to determine if there was an indication of a wedding ring that she might have removed. The thought that she might belong to some man depressed and angered him. And the thought that said man might have harmed or threatened her in some way, forcing her to flee into the wet, cold, dark night, had his blood pounding in his head.

Then he chided himself. Amelia was an anomaly, someone who by speech, manners, and demeanor, clearly came from the upper class, but had the nerve and audacity to wear trousers, leave her home in the rain, climb a tree, and enter an unknown building through the window in the middle of the night. The two scenarios did not gel.

The tea arrived and every subject Driscoll thought to discuss would have sounded like he was questioning her. He didn't realize until now how very difficult it was to have a conversation with someone who was hiding their identity.

Finally, Amelia saved him by asking her own questions. She stirred a bit of sugar into her tea, avoiding his eyes. "You said the Earl of Huntington is your brother. How is it you ended up owning a gambling house?"

Driscoll leaned back in his chair, happy to have an

easy question to answer. "Dante and I, being second and third sons had no expectations of inheriting anything. Hunt—which is what everyone calls the earl—was generous enough to settle a yearly allowance on both of us. However, after a year or so of wasting our time and money, we came up with the idea of buying this club."

"So, it had already been a gaming club when you bought it?"

Driscoll nodded. "Yes. It hadn't been very successful and was subject to numerous raids. Since Hunt has a standing in both the community and the House of Lords, we were pretty sure we could turn the club into a place where the elite in London could go for some gambling fun and not be harassed by the police."

"Since gambling is illegal," Miss Pence said with a slight smirk.

"Hmm. Technically," he smiled. "We approached Hunt about advancing us the money to buy the club outright. The previous owners were anxious to sell, so we got a good deal. We completely renovated the building, added sleeping quarters and a kitchen in the basement and opened for business."

"And have been successful since then."

"Yes. If Scotland Yard plans a raid, which they must do on occasion to avoid too much animosity with those who care about such things, we generally know at least a half hour in advance, which gives us time to close down the gaming part of the room and make it appear as any other gentlemen's club."

Amelia blew on her tea and smiled at him. "Very clever."

Driscoll's jaw dropped at the glorious way her smile lit up her face. His muscles tensed and his body responded by his blood taking a joyful race to his cock. He knew he was in serious trouble.

\* \* \*

THE LITTLE BIT of wine she'd had at dinner along with the wonderful food left Amelia more relaxed than she'd been in a long time. Living with her stepbrother had been fraught with anxiety. Even before Randolph had come to her with his ridiculous demand that she meekly surrender to Lyon's lecherous plans, she'd put up with numerous parties in the house. She would lock herself in her room, terrified someone would attempt to break in.

She'd not felt relaxed or even safe since she left her home in the country. It didn't speak well of her stepbrother that she found security in a gambling club in the middle of London with two men she'd only just met.

"Does your brother, the earl, ever visit the club?"

"Occasionally. Right now, his wife is expecting their first child so he tends to stick close to home."

"Oh, how lovely. They must be very happy." She sighed, thinking about being happily married with her own home and a caring husband. A child would make her life perfect. Right now, it didn't appear that would ever be her life. She had to save money and move as far as possible from London, perhaps even England.

Driscoll covered her hand with his. "What's wrong, Amelia? Won't you tell me? Perhaps I can help."

She was so tempted to turn to this kind man and tell him everything. But she still did not trust him. He might be aghast at her running from the man who was her guardian. Having a guardian at her age was preposterous, but with Randolph holding whatever money his father left, she really had no choice.

"Nothing." She offered him a smile and pulled her hand out from under his. It was best to fight the attraction she felt for Driscoll. She needed to smother the feelings and strange sensations her body experienced when he was near, and grossly stupid to become too attached to this man. Escape was her only option. "Shall we begin work on the books?"

Driscoll looked a bit disappointed that she refused to confide in him, but she couldn't concern herself with that. No longer would she depend on others. Her stepfather had let her down by trusting Randolph, and her stepbrother had done even worse. From now on Amelia would take care of herself.

They walked from the dining room to the office, neither one speaking. The sound of the gaming floor being prepared for the night reached their ears as they walked. Tables readied, furniture polished, carpets being swept. She actually found it exciting. She'd never been a part of something like this. Her life in the country had been quiet.

And safe, she reminded herself.

THEY HAD BEEN at the work for hours on the books and Amelia was certain her eyes were crossed from staring at numbers. They were dry and burning. She rubbed them, but it didn't help. She looked over at Driscoll who still methodically copied numbers from one book to another, looking back and forth. "How do you do this for hours?"

He looked up, almost seeming surprised to see her sitting there. He placed his pencil on the desk and stretched. Her jaw dropped as she stared at him. His muscles flexed under his coat, stretching the seams. For someone who spent a lot of time copying numbers and sitting at a desk, he certainly had quite a nice form.

She closed her mouth and looked down at the desk when he caught her staring at him. Her face flamed when he chuckled.

"Would you like a break, Amelia?"

"Yes, as a matter of fact, I would." She stood,

stretching herself, and was amused to see him staring at her as she'd just been staring at him. Except, instead of his face growing red as hers had, his eyes traveled over her body with a hungry look, making her face flush again.

He waved toward the door and she exited the room. They made their way down the hall to the dining room where a pot of coffee, and one of tea, sat on the sideboard, along with milk, sugar, cups and saucers. An array of biscuits and tarts decorated a silver platter alongside the drinks.

"Is this to keep you awake while you're struggling with all those numbers?" Amelia poured tea into one of the cups.

"It helps." He picked up another cup and filled it with coffee, the steam rising, its bold and lovely scent infusing the air as he poured. She oftentimes wondered why coffee smelled so much better than it tasted.

"If you want something more substantive to eat, there is a buffet table on the game floor. It's where I got your food last night."

She stirred a bit of honey into her tea. "Ah, that was why it hadn't taken you long to fill up a plate. I wondered about that."

They sat at the table where they'd dined a few hours before. Amelia stirred her tea. "I find I am fascinated by this place. I've never seen anything like it—"

"—Which you would not have since ladies are not allowed," Driscoll finished for her.

"Yet, I'm to work in one." Amelia took a sip of tea after blowing on it.

"Yes. However, your identity will be unknown, and therefore, your reputation protected."

"And you believe I have a reputation to protect?"

His brows rose. "Don't you?"

It was time to pull back. If the questions continued,

she would reveal something she'd rather not. She shrugged and sipped more of her tea.

They sat in companionable silence drinking their beverages and listening to the hum of the roulette wheel, the roll of dice, and groans from men who were no doubt on the losing side of a table.

After a while, Amelia turned to ask Driscoll a question and found him staring at her. She'd seen that look before from men she'd met at the few social events she'd attended in the village near her family's country estate.

Her heart sped up and she felt a strange tingle in her middle. She'd never had that reaction to the village men, but Driscoll Rose's heavy-lidded eyes watching her so thoughtfully as he slumped in his chair, his long finger circling the rim of his teacup made her skin feel prickly, as if a lightning storm was approaching.

She licked her dry lips. "What?"

## 7

*D*riscoll knew he had completely lost his grip on common sense as he leaned toward Amelia, cupped her face in his hands and brought his mouth close to hers. "I want to kiss you."

Her eyes grew wide. "Why?"

Since she didn't pull back, instead of answering, he moved the few inches separating them and covered her mouth with his. He nearly moaned with pleasure. Her lips were warm, moist and honey-scented from the tea. He removed his hands from her face to wrap her in his arms, pulling her flush against him.

He'd kissed dozens of women, but none was sweeter, softer, or fit his body so well. He nudged her lips with his tongue, and she smiled, enough movement to gain entry.

To his delight, she slid her hands up his chest and encircled his neck, her slender fingers tugging on the back of his hair. He shifted his mouth to take the kiss deeper, more powerful.

Amelia was sweet in her innocent response to him. Her initial unease faded, and she became more involved with his movements, which to his delight, she mimicked.

The sound of footsteps reluctantly dragged him back to reality. The actuality of where they were and how many people could walk by stopped him cold. If it was his intention to keep Amelia's name free from ruination or scandal, the last thing they needed was to be caught practically pawing at each other in the dining room.

Driscoll pulled back, trying desperately to catch his breath. He glanced over at Amelia who stared at him, her fingers resting on her well-kissed lips. She opened her mouth to speak when Dante strolled into the room.

He glanced at them, then quickly offered Driscoll a smirk that he hoped with all his being Amelia had not seen.

"I thought you two were working on the books." He reached for the coffee pot and poured himself a cup.

"We're taking a break," Driscoll snapped.

Dante turned and took a seat across from Amelia. "A break? Is that what you call it now?"

Driscoll rose from his seat, his heart pounding in his chest. His hands balled into fists that he was prepared to use on his brother's grinning mouth. "Yes, a break. Amelia and I have been staring at numbers for hours. We deserve a break."

His brother held his hands up in surrender. "All right. I only asked. I never remember you taking a break that involved leaving your desk." He nodded at Amelia. "Very dedicated, my brother."

She raised her chin and stared at Dante. "Yes. I know he is dedicated. You are fortunate to have a partner such as him."

She was beautiful in the flush that remained on her face. Either from their short bout of passion, or her anger at his brother. Either way she reminded him of a female warrior.

"I totally agree, Miss Pence." Dante lowered his

voice almost as if in repentance, which Driscoll in no way believed. "Driscoll is a fine partner. And brother."

"It's time we returned to work," Driscoll said as he pulled out Amelia's chair.

"In all seriousness, Driscoll, I do need a few minutes of your time. A few issues have come up that we need to discuss."

"Of course, do you want to go over them now?"

Amelia walked to the doorway. "I will return to work."

Once she was gone, Driscoll took his seat. "What issues are there?"

"Remember Lord Randolph Newton?" Dante took a sip of coffee.

"The one we banned for fighting?"

"The very same."

Driscoll snorted. "The man is an idiot, and ready to raise his fists for the slightest reason. Why are you bringing him up now?"

"He appeared at the door tonight with one of his friends, Mr. Daniel Lyons, who is still a member, but close to being banned himself for cheating at cards."

Driscoll frowned. "If he was caught cheating at cards why hasn't he already been banned?"

"Because it wasn't proven, just strongly suggested by one club member. A Lord Batterley."

"I know the man. He's accused more than one member of cheating. In fact, he cornered me at White's one afternoon with a long recitation of two other members he believed filched money from him in card games."

Dante shook his head. "It seems Newton showed up here with Lyons in an attempt to be reinstated."

"What did you tell him?"

"I said I would speak with you about it. My own opinion is we should keep him banned. There's something shady about the man that I don't like. What I wanted to know from you is how much is he in debt to us?"

Driscoll thought for a moment. "I would have to check my books. I don't think it's an outstanding amount or I would know right off how much. Come with me to the office and I'll check." He stood. "Was there anything else you wanted to discuss?"

"Yes." Dante drained his coffee cup and set it down. "Have you learned anything else about our new employee? It seemed when I entered that the two of you have become—shall we say—friendly?"

Driscoll gritted his teeth. "Don't. Say. Any. More."

Dante shrugged. "I don't care one way or the other, except we don't know anything more about the woman now than we did the night she dropped through the window."

"What is your concern, then?"

They began to walk back to the office. "Nothing really. Curious, perhaps. Unless she gives me reason to believe there is something in whatever her secret is that she's keeping that could hurt us." He glanced over at Driscoll. "Or you."

"Don't worry about me, little brother. I can take care of myself."

\* \* \*

AMELIA RAISED her head as Driscoll and Dante entered the office. She'd been a little concerned when Dante said he wanted to speak with his brother. As she worked on transferring numbers, questions plagued her. Had they found out who she was? Did Randolph manage to track her down? Was she about to be fired and tossed onto the street? Or, horrors, were they about to turn her over to her stepbrother?

Although she did not truly trust them, from what she'd seen she doubted that either brother would condone her stepbrother selling her into prostitution. But who knew what sort of a story Randolph would spin for them? Men were always believed over women.

As she worked, she had also tried to make sense of the kiss she and Driscoll had shared. She would be lying to herself if she pretended it was a complete surprise. She'd felt the attraction between them, even from the time she crawled through his window.

At one and twenty years she had experienced a few kisses from the village boys, but absolutely nothing like she just shared with Driscoll. Her blood was still running hot and she'd yet to get her breathing completely under control.

Her social life had been scant. She'd been able to attend some of the local assemblies while she still had her companion, Mrs. Marsh. But in the past year Randolph had dismissed the woman, saying Amelia was too old for a companion since she was considered a spinster. She always felt he let Mrs. Marsh go because he didn't want to pay her wages anymore. Once she lacked a chaperon, attending dances was no longer possible.

The brothers walked past the desk where she worked to a cabinet where Driscoll pulled out another ledger. He placed it on his desk and flipped a few pages. "It looks like Newton is into us for about ten pounds."

Amelia's breath caught. *Newton?* Could they possibility be speaking of her stepbrother? A chill ran down her spine and she broke into a sweat.

"Not a considerable amount, but certainly noteworthy." Dante leaned back on the edge of the desk, his arms crossed over his chest. "I'm still concerned about the fighting, though."

Oh my lord! It had to be Randolph. Were they considering allowing him back into the club? Even with a mask she was sure he would recognize her, especially if he sat at the vingt-et-un table, staring at her as she dealt cards. She had visions of him ripping off her mask and dragging her out of the club kicking and screaming.

"I agree. I think the ban should continue."

Relief swept through Amelia so strong she almost cried. Her hands shook as she attempted to write numbers. Luckily neither brother was paying her any attention.

"If Lyons shows up with Newton again, tell him he is welcome, but Newton is not."

"Were they turned away already?"

"Yes. The rule is if you're banned it matters not who you show up with, the ban stands. Now that we've decided to keep it in place, I will send a note around to Newton and tell him the bad news."

They then continued to go over the list of members who owed money and for how long, commenting that luckily the outstanding debts were not unmanageable. Dante took his leave shortly after their conversation.

Driscoll looked over at her, but she ignored him. She didn't want to discuss the kiss since she was still reeling from the fact that Randolph had come close to being readmitted back into the Rose Room.

She looked up when Driscoll's shadow fell over her desk. "Amelia?"

"Yes?"

"You seem upset. I didn't want to say anything when Dante was here, but I noticed your hand shaking."

She waved him off. "'Tis nothing."

He rested his hip on her desk and swung his foot. "I want you to know Amelia, that you can trust me. If there is some sort of danger you are in, please let me know. I would protect you, but I need to know what I'm protecting you from."

She attempted a smile. "No danger. I think I'm merely tired."

He studied her carefully. "Are you upset because I kissed you?"

It took her a moment, then she said, "No. I mean, I was not upset, maybe a little bit surprised."

"I think you feel the same attraction between us that I do. If not, just say so and I will never bother you again." He reached out and brushed back an errant curl behind her ear.

She chewed on her lip. Of course, she felt the attraction. How could she avoid it every time she looked into this man's deep brown eyes?

"May I be honest?"

Driscoll's shoulders stiffened. "Of course."

She stood and walked around the desk, unable to sit with him so close and think clearly. She fiddled with her dress, folding the fabric, then smoothing it out. "I won't deny the attraction." She blushed and he smiled. "However, I am not in a place where I can encourage the attention of a man. Any man."

"Ah, Amelia." He studied her for a minute, then continued. "It comes down to trust, does it not? You don't trust me, and in truth, we have not known each other long enough for trust to develop."

He reached out and took her hand, drawing her close to him. "Will you allow me to try?"

She almost cried with frustration. Were she in any other place and time she would love to have the attentions of this man. He was handsome, charming, helpful, and caring. He and his brother ran a successful business which would provide a nice living for a wife and children.

But she would never be that wife. Once Randolph found out where she was, he would use his guardianship to bring her back home and then pass her on to Daniel Lyons.

"I don't think it would work." She drew herself up

and fought the tears in her eyes. "I'm sorry." Her voice shook. "But, no."

Before she could change her mind or collapse into a bundle of tears against his strong chest, she backed up and headed toward the door. "I think I will retire for the night. I am quite tired."

He didn't move from his spot, didn't try to stop her, but continued to watch her as she made her quick escape.

She wasn't sure if that was a good thing or a bad thing.

---

## 8

*R*andolph Newton slammed his empty whiskey glass on the table, barely avoiding the edge of the table, and swore. "*Bloody hell*, where did the bitch disappear to?"

His drinking partner, well into his cups himself, shrugged. "Her disappearance is not my problem. 'Tis yours, my friend. You owe me."

Newton glowered at him. "I thought you were so anxious to get between her thighs, Lyons."

He nodded. "I am. But it is your responsibility to deliver her to me. I will give you three days. Then I will demand payment in coin."

"I don't have the blunt. You know that. And you agreed to take Amelia in payment."

Lyons stretched his arms out, almost toppling from his chair. "Do I see her here, Newton? Is she sitting on my lap, Newton? Has she warmed my bed yet, Newton? A man can't enjoy the pleasures of his mistress if she is missing, Newton."

Newton shook his head. "She has no friends in London. She has no money to travel back to the family estate. And even if she did, it's already occupied." He ran his fingers through his already-tousled hair.

"Where could she go? It doesn't make sense." He shook his head and poured more whiskey into his glass, spilling part of it on the table.

Lyons held out his own glass which Newton refilled.

They both sat brooding while they consumed their drinks. "Another annoyance," Newton said, "is the bloody Rose brothers. Who the bloody hell do they think they are, banning me from their club? Do they know who I am?"

"Clearly, if you're on their banned list."

Newton scowled. "Fights happen all the time in those places."

"According to the brute they have at the door, not at The Rose Room." Lyons hiccupped.

"Damn aristocrats. And that last brother is a bastard. Where does he get off banning me," Newton pounded on his chest, "a member of the nobility? I am Viscount Newton. He is nothing. A bastard, a by-blow, born on the wrong side of the blanket."

Daniel examined his glass which was empty again. He shrugged, glanced at the empty bottle and placed the glass on the table. "Might be a bastard, but the old earl raised him with the other two. Nothing puts foolish ideas into a man's head more than being treated as an equal to his betters."

"Hah! Someone needs to bring the bastard down a peg."

Just as Newton settled in, thinking a nap would do well right then, Daniel asked, "What are you going to do about your sister?"

Newton's eyes popped open, and he slammed his glass down again. "Find her. Find the bitch and give her a well-deserved beating before I turn her over to you."

Daniel shrugged. "Just don't damage the chit. I like her beautiful face just the way it is, and I don't want to wait to shag her while she heals from injuries." He leaned forward, grabbing the table to keep from falling.

"Just make it quick. The girl or the blunt so I can buy another one."

\* \* \*

DRISCOLL SMILED at Amelia as she entered the dining room in time for breakfast. He was still brooding about her rejection the night before, but decided not to push her, and allow her time. Time for them to discover each other and for now just be his employee.

For now.

He did not mean to give up. There was something about her that touched a part of him of which he'd been unaware. He liked the feeling, but at the same time knew he had to go slow. No woman had ever captured his interest for more than a few nights in his bed the way she did. Since he was treading in unknown territory, it was best to give Amelia time to trust him.

He knew there was something she was running from, possibly dangerous, and he was not mistaken that something had upset her last night. He tried to remember what he and Dante had been talking about at the time, but all he recalled was going over the names and numbers of those indebted to the club.

He stood and pulled out a chair for her. "Good morning, Amelia." It occurred to him that most likely Margie had only purchased one dress and she certainly could not wear that every day. "For as lovely as that frock is, I do believe you will need more than one. In fact, there might be other things that she did not purchase for you. Can I escort you to Bond Street to do some shopping this morning?"

At first, she sucked in a deep breath, her face growing pale, beginning to shake her head, then she stopped and seemed to reconsider. "Yes. Actually, if you don't mind advancing more of my wages, there are some other things I could use."

He was quite surprised that she was willing to go out in public but was happy to oblige. "Excellent. After we eat, we can take the carriage to Bond Street."

She smiled and his heart took an extra thump. He quickly attempted to rein in his enthusiasm. Until he knew more about Amelia, he really needed to keep his heart protected.

They enjoyed their breakfast with his new employee admitting she was both anxious and excited to begin training for her job. She let slip that she'd never held a job before which was no surprise since he'd already classified her as a lady. It still confused him as to why he did not know her. At least by name. But he was not at all familiar with a Pence family.

That was another reason to believe she had given him a false name. But she was willing to accompany him to Bond Street, so he might file that information away for future consideration.

Amelia wiped her mouth with her napkin and placed it alongside her place. "If you will give me a minute, I will join you downstairs for our trip."

"I shall be waiting on the game room floor. It's about time you paid a visit to where you will be working."

*  *  *

AMELIA HURRIED AWAY from Driscoll and headed to the bedroom to retrieve her hat. An outdated bonnet, it was one she'd borrowed from a maid. She had been grateful to Margie for buying her the few items she had, but as a lady, Amelia felt she was not properly dressed to go out without a hat and gloves, neither of which Margie purchased.

She'd almost fainted from anxiety when Driscoll first mentioned going on a shopping trip, until she remembered Randolph and his cohorts never rose before the sun was about to set. She had plenty of time to visit stores and buy a few things without the fear of being recognized. A few more items would make her life easier while she stayed at the club.

After adjusting the sorry hat, smoothing her hair, pinching her cheeks and biting her lips--she didn't know why—yes, she did—she left to meet Driscoll downstairs.

Her first glimpse of the game floor overwhelmed her. Even with the staff cleaning up from the night before, and the club empty of members, it still left her a bit giddy. She wove her way through the gaming tables, apologizing to the people who were cleaning and straightening up. They were a friendly group, all of them offering her a smile.

Although she hadn't noticed at first, it eventually came to her attention that a few of the female employees dipped a curtsey to her. How did they know?

When she thought on it, her place in society would be apparent. She'd been born Lady Amelia, daughter of the Marquess of Salisbury. Her mother had raised her daughter in the manner that behooved the station to which she'd been born, which meant a governess to teach her, and tutors for other things necessary for a lady. Young Amelia had also been trained in deportment, watercolors, embroidery, pianoforte, and dancing. All had been in expectation of making her way into London Society at the appropriate time.

Then her mother died when Amelia was thirteen years. Money that should have come to her and her mother was used to pay the tremendous debts her father had accrued in his lifetime. The entailed properties passed to a young cousin who never made an appearance in all the time she and her mother lived there after her father's death.

After a decent year of mourning, Mother married

Lord Newton, who took a liking to Amelia. However, after Mother died, he went into a decline, leaving Amelia to her own resources. He never arranged for the debut her mother had prepared her for, and passed away two years ago, consigning her to Randolph's clutches.

"The carriage is in front when you are ready," Driscoll said. He'd come up behind her without her even noticing.

She spun around, feeling like a young girl. She waved her arms in the air. "This is incredible! I've never been in a club before."

"Nor should you have been." Driscoll frowned at her. "This is not the place for ladies."

Feeling quite cheerful, she took his arm and they headed out the front door. "Yet, I am to work in one."

"That is a good reminder that we must find you a mask to wear before you begin working."

"Do you know where to find such things?" Amelia took Driscoll's offered hand and stepped up into the carriage.

"I do. We run a masquerade ball once a year and Dante and I are forced to wear a mask those evenings."

The carriage started up with a jerk. "What use is a ball if ladies aren't allowed?"

"That one night a year they are permitted to attend. But we close down the gaming tables and only have an orchestra, food and dancing."

"How wonderful!" She could hear the excitement in her voice. "When is the next one?"

"Actually, it's next month. We hold it in October so we don't interfere with those who travel to their country estates for the holiday season."

"Are the employees permitted to attend?"

Driscoll nodded. "Yes, indeed. A few of the more high-in-the-instep ladies of the *ton* don't approve, but we've always felt that they had the option to stay home if that troubles them so much."

"You are a good man, Driscoll Rose." She leaned over and patted his knee, then quickly removed her hand when his eyes darkened, and he offered a slight smile. She drew in a deep breath and looked out the window. It was best to keep her hands where they belonged. And they did not belong on Driscoll's person.

* * *

THE FIRST STORE they visited was the famous Fenwick's. Amelia acted so innocently excited, glancing around like she was in a castle, touching the items for sale almost with reverence, that he presumed she had never been there before. Another strange piece of the puzzle that was his new employee.

Driscoll left her to seek the store manager and discretely arrange to have the bills for all her purchases sent to him, less they start any rumors of her being his mistress.

He soon realized that no matter where they went no one seemed to know her. Although he would hardly consider himself active in Society, it appeared with Amelia alongside him, everyone he'd ever met wanted to speak with him, while casting speculative sideway glances at his companion.

He introduced her by merely mentioning her name, never offering more, since he had no idea what to say. He certainly couldn't divulge she was one of his employees. He'd thought about saying she was his cousin but as a youth he'd learned that lies eventually came back to haunt one.

The thought crossed his mind that despite his arrangement with the store manager, and the fact that they were out together without a chaperone, it still might be assumed she was his mistress, but he relied on her natural grace and behavior to mark her as a lady.

However, no doubt many Londoners were left with questions about the young lady accompanying Driscoll Rose on a shopping spree. He cringed, hoping such question would not appear in the society column of the next day's newspaper.

Another proof of Amelia's unfamiliarity with London Society was her oblivion to how it looked for the two of them being together, shopping. Since she lacked sophistication, he should have been the one to think of that before they'd ventured out.

With the damage already done, they ended their foray to the shops with a visit to Gunter's for tea. All her purchases were tidily stacked in the carriage or had been arranged for delivery.

"I can't tell you how happy I am to have a few pieces of clothing." She stirred her tea and looked over at him, then studied her cup. "I know you are wondering why I arrived at your club with nothing but the clothes on my back."

Truth be told his major question was why no one knew her. However, there didn't seem to be any point in pursuing that since he'd already reconciled himself to the fact that she would only tell him what she wanted him to know when she was ready. If that day ever came. He shrugged and didn't respond, and she seemed to accept that, and in fact looked quite relieved.

However, as they enjoyed their tea, he thought about the conundrum that was Miss Pence. And what in the world he was to do about her.

## 9

"*I*'m telling you, Dante, it was a surreal experience. No matter where we went, no one knew Amelia. Everyone seemed anxious to meet her, and there was certainly speculation in their eyes, but absolutely no recognition. From anyone."

"That seems almost impossible." Dante shook his head. "It's very obvious the girl is a lady. Everything about her screams Upper Crust. That girl has been born and bred to wed a gentleman of the *ton*, run his household with ease and aplomb, and raise his heirs. I'd bet tonight's winnings on that."

"I agree. She told me she is one and twenty years which means she should have had her come-out a few years ago. Even if she was buried in the country, does she have no relatives? No one who would have at least made the usual rounds with the girl since she's here now in London? Parties, balls, musicales." Driscoll took another sip of his coffee.

"Even though she dropped through the window with nothing but the clothes on her back, she had to come from somewhere. I'm willing to bet someone is searching for her," Dante said.

Driscoll studied his brother. "Someone she doesn't want to find her."

"Yet she's willing to work here at the club where hundreds of people visit weekly."

"But, as I pointed out at the beginning of this conversation, no one we met in London knew her. And, she will be wearing a mask that will cover most of her face."

Dante finished his coffee and stood. "Someone knows her, or she wouldn't be running." He slapped Driscoll on the shoulder. "Time to go to work. Are you training with Amelia tonight?"

"Yes. We're going to go over vingt-et-un a few times with just the two of us and then I will have a few other staff members join in."

Dante headed to the door. "Marcus is anxious to get off the vingt-et-un table and work as security. The sooner you get Amelia trained, the quicker we can make that switch."

"She is a smart woman. I don't think it will take her long to be comfortable."

Driscoll left the dining room and headed to the bedroom Amelia was currently using. He knocked softly and she immediately opened the door.

He would never get used to looking at her without the reaction she caused. She wore one of the ready-made dresses they'd purchased earlier. The deep rose taffeta set off her blonde hair and blue eyes. The neck-line was just right. Not low enough to distract the players—although that might be a good thing—and high enough to show her status as a proper young lady.

Amelia offered him a slight dip and a bright smile. The only indication of her nervousness was her hands which she clasped firmly in front of her. She took in a deep breath, immediately drawing his eyes to the creamy skin above her neckline. "I'm ready."

His mouth dropped and he quickly coughed to

cover his reaction. He had the strange urge to extend his elbow and parade her down the corridor like they were arriving at a ball. He mentally shook himself and merely waved her forward. "I thought we would practice in the dining room for a while. Then when you are comfortable, I will ask some of the staff to join us."

She licked her lips and nodded, her eyes growing wide. "That is a good idea." The strangled words coming from her plump lips belied their truth. Of course, she would be nervous. She was not raised to work in a gaming club.

But she presented a dilemma. They could not toss her into the street, and if she were to stay here under their protection, she had to earn her keep to avoid any gossip. And no, he answered his wicked thoughts, she would not earn her keep that way.

Once Amelia finally decided to trust him enough to reveal what she was all about, he wanted to make sure her reputation remained intact. Of course, working in a gaming club wasn't exactly keeping her name pure, but at least if she appeared to be merely another employee, she might avoid the worst of it.

*Or I could marry her and completely save her reputation.*

Where the bloody hell did that come from? Marriage? Could he be serious? It wasn't as if the wedded state was something he was against, but with his limited social life it didn't seem he would marry any time soon. At least he hadn't spent a great deal of time thinking about it. Until. . .

*She dropped into my life.*

*Maybe it's fate.*

Or maybe he needed to alter his thinking and get on with training his new employee. He knew nothing about her. No one in London knew her. For all he knew she could be running from a husband. He glanced at her left hand again, reassuring himself there was no wedding ring, or the impression of one that she might have taken off.

No, until she trusted him with the information about herself, he and his brother were doing enough to help her in whatever situation from which she was escaping.

He held her chair out and took the one across from her. Time to concentrate on what they were here for. He pulled the deck of cards from his pocket and began to shuffle.

"Since you are familiar with the game, I won't have to instruct you on how to proceed, but merely play a few hands so you can get the feel of the cards, the game, and playing against someone."

She nodded and took another deep breath. Lord save him from leaping across the table and covering her sweet plump lips with his. It was time to concentrate on the game. Not on the woman.

About an hour passed as they played the game, alternating between him and Amelia as 'the dealer.' He could see her confidence grow as the time passed.

As he'd told Dante, she was a smart woman, and he could see how quickly she mimicked his movements and studied her own hand as well as his. She started out cautiously, but after a while she grew more confident and began to take chances.

They finished a hand, and he pulled the cards together and began to shuffle. "Are you ready to have a few other people join us? You would be the dealer."

"Yes. I think I'm ready." She grinned and he couldn't help but return her smile.

"I'll be right back. Why don't you ring for something to drink, or eat if you're hungry?"

"I could use some tea. But I hate to ring for it. I'm just another employee."

She had a good point. Resentment might build if she was given privileges others were not. It was bad enough that she slept in the bedroom on the office floor. "I agree. I will have someone from the kitchen send up tea when I go down to find a few employees to join us."

Driscoll made his way to the kitchen, requested the tea and then found some employees to join him and Amelia upstairs. Since he was away from his desk—which was a rarity—he strolled the game floor for a while. It appeared the house was doing quite well tonight.

"Well, good evening, Mr. Rose. We rarely see you down here." Mrs. Beckenridge patted him on the arm with the painted fan dangling from her wrist. The widow was notorious for switching lovers at an alarming rate. She apparently was so experienced and so willing to delve into anything and everything that the line was long to replace her current lover.

She'd teased him just about every time they'd met, but there was absolutely nothing about the woman that tempted him. Why she continued to goad him was beyond comprehension. He'd never given her any indication that she was of interest to him. Unless it was his resistance that held appeal. Perhaps she couldn't stand the thought of a man not eager to take her to his bed.

Not that he was a prude, but he didn't care for the idea of having a well-used woman underneath him. Aside from the possibility of picking up a disease, he was much more select in choosing his partners.

Nevertheless, she was a patron, and he had a job to do and a business to run. "Good evening to you as well, Mrs. Beckenridge. I thought it time to take a break and look around, so I don't forget what the place looks like." He grinned hoping that was enough conversation for her. He went to move past her, and she reached out and grasped his upper arm.

"You spend far too much time with your nose buried in your ledgers." She ran her long, red fingernail from his shoulder down his arm. "I can offer you something much more interesting to bury your nose in."

Good God, the woman had no shame. He was almost embarrassed for her, even though she only smiled at what she must have thought was a much-coveted invitation. His skin crawled and he couldn't get away fast enough. "Some other time, perhaps." He bowed and moved as fast as he could.

The sound of her deep, sultry laugh followed him.

"Watch out for that one." Dante nodded in Mrs. Beckenridge's direction as he strolled up to Driscoll.

"No need to warn me, brother. She holds no appeal, I assure you." Driscoll shook his head in disgust and headed back upstairs, making a wide circle around Mrs. Beckenridge.

* * *

AMELIA PLAYED a game of solitaire as she waited for Driscoll and the staff members he was bringing with him. She'd always enjoyed the game, especially when she was tense and unable to lose herself in a book.

Just about the entire time she'd spent with her stepbrother.

In the couple months since she'd relocated from her much beloved home in the country to his townhouse in London, she'd been on edge. It had been apparent from the start that he had no intention of introducing her to London Society. When she asked him about a Season and told him she knew her stepfather had planned one for her, he laughed.

The former Lord Newton had been very different from his son. Although her stepfather had lost interest in just about everything after Amelia's mother died, he did tell her that one day he would take her to London, find someone to sponsor her, have a come-out, find a husband and have the life she was born and raised to have.

That never happened and she was left alone. Until Randolph summoned her and she was naive enough to think it was for the purpose of honoring his father's promises. She should have known better.

Driscoll entered the dining room with Margie and two of the security guards. Right behind him was Betsy rolling a tea cart. She placed the items on the sideboard, then pushed the cart to the corner of the room and took a seat at the table, grinning at Amelia.

Looking for a little bit of fortification before the game, Amelia walked to the sideboard and looked over at Driscoll. "Would you like tea?"

He nodded and she proceeded to pour and fix his tea precisely as he liked it since she'd seen him do it many times before. She did not offer to any of the others because they were fellow employees, not the employer as Driscoll was.

She smiled to herself. Even in such strange surroundings she still held fast to the manners she was taught by her governess and tutors. If only all she had learned had been put to its proper use.

As much as she longed for the life she had planned, right now she was grateful to have a place to sleep, food to eat, and a job that would pay her money so she could one day make her escape completely from London and far away from Randolph.

She stirred her tea until it cooled as the others filled their teacups and filled plates with the small sandwiches, biscuits and tarts the kitchen had sent up. They all engaged in conversation as they enjoyed the repast. She was fascinated at how involved in the club the employees were. Apparently, the Rose brothers were such good employers that their staff felt as though they were part of the business.

Eventually all the tea things were cleared away by

Margie, and Driscoll handed her two decks of cards. "We use two, and sometimes three decks, at the table, depending on how many are playing. It keeps the dealer from having to constantly reshuffle and makes it harder for players to count cards."

She nodded, took a deep breath, shuffled the two decks and dealt to each participant.

After a few mishaps when each player assured her she was doing fine, she fell into a rhythm. Over an hour passed before she realized it. She had a nice stack of chips—black tin circles they'd played with in place of money—which she'd gathered from those who had lost to her.

Driscoll held up his hand as she prepared to shuffle again. "I think that is enough for tonight."

Amelia hadn't realized how tense she'd been throughout the session until Driscoll spoke. All her muscles relaxed, and she drew in a deep breath. She glanced over at him to see his reaction to how she played.

He smiled that crooked smile that she liked so much and pushed his spectacles up on his nose. "You did a fine job tonight. I think only one more practice session and you will be ready to take over Marcus's table."

"Is Marcus leaving?" Betsy asked.

"No. He wants to move into a security position. It was fortunate that Miss Pence arrived when she did to replace him. It saved us from having to hire someone that we did not know."

Of course, no one mentioned that Amelia was someone they didn't know. Not all knew exactly how she arrived at the club, but it was known that there was a story behind her presence.

So far Amelia had remained separate from the other employees, but she hoped to change that once she began working. She did not like living and eating detached from the others. She did not want any special

71

attention. Special attention could cause envy, which could lead to a disgruntled employee possibly uncovering her secret and selling the information to Randolph.

Slowly, all the employees rose and headed out of the dining room. Amelia checked the clock on the wall and was surprised to see it was already two o'clock in the morning.

Exhaustion hit her like a steam engine. She actually stumbled as she stood. Driscoll caught her around the waist, and she was grateful that all the employees had left. The last thing she needed, to prevent any idea of her having special privileges, was seeing Driscoll's arm wrapped around her.

"I'm fine," she said and moved away from him. Driscoll immediately moved his arm.

"I will walk you to your room."

She shook her head. "No. That's not necessary."

"Ah, but it is. You are very tired and probably worn out from working so hard. It's my gentlemanly duty to see you to your door."

"Oh, for goodness sake. You make it sound as though my room is miles away and we're courting." She immediately felt the blush start in her center and make its way up her face. Especially when Driscoll studied her carefully, as if looking for something.

The corridor was lit by gaslight sconces on the walls. They moved from dark to light several times and Amelia's heart went from normal to pounding by the time they reached her door. This was foolish. She had nothing to concern herself with.

They reached her door and she turned to thank him when he leaned his forearm against the door frame and towered over her. He ran his finger down her cheek. "May I kiss you goodnight, Miss Pence?"

## 10

*D*riscoll decided he must be bloody out of his mind. But it appeared his body had ignored his brain and continued to desire this woman who no one seemed to know anything about.

When Amelia hadn't answered his request for a kiss, but hadn't denied it either, or entered her room to shut the door in his face, Driscoll bent slowly, giving her a chance to retreat. When his lips met hers, he came alive at the pleasure of tasting her once again, feeling her warmth, inhaling the scent of lavender and Amelia.

He nudged her lips with his tongue, and she opened, cautiously at first, then used her own tongue to taste him. She pressed her body against his and moaned softly.

After almost a full minute of pleasure, Driscoll pulled away and scattered kisses along her jawline, on the soft skin under her ear. "I want you so much, Amelia. Do you have any idea what you do to me? I'm tortured with the idea of you sleeping here, so very near to my office."

He smoothed his palms up her arms and cupped her face, turning her head to take her lips once again, going deeper, demanding surrender. With a slight moan from deep in her chest, Amelia wrapped her arms around his waist and ran her hands over his back.

Reluctantly, Driscoll pulled back and stared at her. Amelia's face was flushed, and her eyes slowly drifted open. The only sound to be heard was the panting coming from the two of them as they attempted to regain control.

He leaned his forehead against hers. "I must go now," he whispered as he slowly tucked a loose curl behind her ear. He could not push her any further. And he would never compromise a woman under his employ, nor would he dally with a well-bred young lady who must save her virtue for her husband.

*Husband.*

He took a deep breath. Until he knew more about her, her background, and what she as running from he could not go down that path. He needed to bide his time and get to know her better.

Have her trust him.

He bent and kissed the top of her head. "Good night, Amelia." Before he could change his mind, he strode determinedly from the overwhelming temptation, down the corridor, and entered his office.

'Twas too bad he didn't keep brandy in his office. Making a decision completely unlike him, he left the office and took the stairs to the game floor.

The noise and confusion that usually raised his spirits did nothing except encourage him in his quest for a drink.

"Good evening, Driscoll. Am I to believe you are here for a drink?" Stephen, the man serving the bar that evening grinned.

"Yes." Driscoll ran his fingers through his hair. "It's been one of those nights."

Stephen poured a brandy into a snifter and set it before Driscoll. "I heard you were training the new girl who is taking over for Marcus. Was the session so difficult, then?"

Driscoll downed half the drink in one gulp. "No." He coughed, as the brandy took his breath away. "Not at all. She is very clever, and I expect Miss Pence to be able to relieve Marcus this week."

"That's good. I know he's ready to move into the security spot," Stephen said.

They chatted for a few minutes, discussing the upcoming yearly ball and the preparations needed. Dante joined them and motioned for Stephen to pour him a drink.

"How did the training go?" his brother asked as he swirled his brandy in the snifter.

"Very well. Amelia is bright as we've noted before. She was a tad nervous at the start, but by the end of the session she was quite confident."

Dante nodded. "Good. We could use her tomorrow."

"Already?"

"Yes. Miles must travel to his home in Yorkshire for his mother's funeral. Marcus can step into his place and Amelia can take over the vingt-et-un table." He raised his cut crystal glass to take a sip and stopped. "Unless you think she can't do it. I don't want to put too much pressure on the girl."

"I think she can do it. Perhaps I can stay close to her for a little while to offer support."

Dante grinned as only his brother could. "Stay close to her, eh?" He finished his drink and slammed the glass down onto the bar. "Whatever you need to do." With a smirk and a slight salute, he strolled away, chuckling.

Blasted brothers. Why did he need them?

Stephen was busy handing out complimentary drinks to members, so Driscoll sauntered over to the vingt-et-un table to watch the game for a while.

Marcus was indeed competent, and dealt the hands

with ease, and a touch of boredom. It was truly time to move him into security.

With training Amelia, he hadn't done anything with the books, so he made his way upstairs to the office. He raised the flame on the gas lamp on the wall by the door and headed to his desk.

He pulled out two ledgers and drew the stack of IOUs toward him. Most of the members arrived with enough blunt to see them through the night, but there were always those who gambled beyond what they'd brought or didn't have enough to begin with and thought they'd make it up at the tables.

Even though he and his brothers owned a gaming club, he'd never been a gambler himself. As a young man fresh from University, he'd done his share of gambling, drinking and whoring, but soon determined there was nothing to be had for him in such a life.

What he never understood was how a man could gamble away his fortune, and in some cases, everything he owned that wasn't entailed. As a general rule, they would usually escort a man out of the building if it looked like he was getting in way over his head. But in the end, they were running a business and that business was gambling. If a man wanted to throw his money away, he would just as easily do it at another club.

Numbers did not interest him enough tonight. Not with the picture in his mind of Amelia warm and soft and lying in a bed only a few doors away. He slammed the book shut and left the office again.

Thank heavens the night was almost over.

* * *

AMELIA TURNED IN HER BED, crossed her hands over her middle, and stared at the canopy overhead. By the looks of the sun coming through the window it must have been close to noontime. Although Driscoll had left her at her door a little after two o'clock that morning, it was nearer to five before she fell asleep.

She'd spent a great deal of time tossing and turning in the bed. At first her body was simply uncomfortable. She ached in places of which she was generally unaware. Her nipples were sensitive and the area between her legs was heavy and moist.

Then once that had passed, her brain deliberated repetitively on the kiss she and Driscoll had shared at the door.

*I want you so much, Amelia. Do you have any idea what you do to me? I'm tortured with the idea of you sleeping here, so very near to my office.*

She shivered each time those words replayed in her head. It troubled her immensely that, had Driscoll continued his assault, she might have invited him into the bedroom.

Whatever had she been thinking?

The last thing she needed was that complication. Her life had never been in such turmoil. She needed to remember her plan. Save money. Leave London. Start a new life. Driscoll Rose had no part in that plan. She still wasn't absolutely certain that he, or Dante, would not turn her over to Randolph had they discovered her situation.

She was amazed at how her trust in humans had shrunk since her own stepbrother had offered her up as payment for a debt. Since her contact with men had been quite limited, she had no idea if that was the way most of them behaved. Until she was sure, she intended to stick with her plan, and put Driscoll far from her mind.

And heart.

She threw off the covers and gave herself a wash in the water that was quite cold from the night before. Since Randolph had fired her companion, there had been no chocolate in the morning, no warm water to wash with, and no assistance in dressing and fixing her hair.

Those were pleasantries she might as well get used to no longer enjoying. She doubted very much if she could ever save enough, or earn enough, to employ servants.

At least she had a roof over her head and food on the table and a way to earn money. She had none of that and no way to secure it when she'd snuck out the window of Randolph's townhouse with no more than the clothes on her back.

When she gave herself time to ponder what she'd done, it amazed her that things had worked out as well as they had.

Once she was washed and dressed, she made her way to the dining room. Both Dante and Driscoll stood as she entered. She glanced briefly at Driscoll and felt the flush rise to her face.

Dante smirked and Driscoll glared at him.

"Good morning." Driscoll pulled out a chair for her.

"Good morning." She nodded at Dante and Driscoll. The teapot sat on the table so she helped herself to tea.

"I have good news for you," Driscoll said as he poured more coffee into his cup.

She smiled at him and he hesitated. "What is that?"

He cleared his throat. "You will work this evening at the vingt-et-un table."

Amelia almost dropped her teacup. "Tonight? Do you think I'm ready?" Any desire she'd had for breakfast fled.

Driscoll reached over and covered her hand with his. "Yes. You are ready. You did a wonderful job yesterday."

She swallowed her fear. "Why so soon?"

Dante leaned back in his chair and crossed his arms over his chest. "One of the security men has to take some time off for a family matter and Marcus is taking his position. So, you will be taking Marcus's place."

She blew out a deep breath. Well, she had no choice. They had been more than good to her. She could not let them down. "Yes. I think I will be all right." She just wished her words were more forceful.

"Driscoll will stay close to the table for the first hour or so for moral support." Dante stood and nodded to her. "I am off to visit a friend—"

Driscoll snorted.

"—I will see you later."

Once Dante left, Amelia stood and put food on her plate from the sideboard. She couldn't starve herself all day in anticipation of working that night. She sucked in a breath as she suddenly remembered something. "I don't have a mask!"

The words came out with almost a hysterical tone. She really needed to calm herself.

"It's all right, Amelia, I have a few in my office that I mentioned we used for our annual ball. When you are finished eating, we can pull them out and see which one suits you."

"Oh, yes. I remember you saying that." She took her seat again and tried her best to smile. "I might be a tad nervous."

Driscoll grinned. "That is understandable."

He didn't seem willing to speak about the kiss from the night before, so she kept silent on it and began to eat her breakfast.

Driscoll stood and pushed in his chair. "I have some work that needs to be done if I am to have the time to spend on the floor tonight."

Amelia looked up at him. "I can help you." She smiled and noticed again he seemed to hesitate. "If you are going to help me, it only seems fair."

He nodded. "Yes. That is a good idea. Well, then I will see you when your breakfast is finished."

* * *

Driscoll strode to the office and threw himself into his chair, his legs stretched out, his fingers linked, resting on his stomach. He'd pretty much convinced himself that his infatuation with Amelia was just that. An infatuation. Nothing more. Something he would soon get over.

Then one look at her this morning, one smile from her lips and he was back to where he'd started. She fascinated him. She made him smile, made his days seem better and brighter than his days had been for quite some time. He wanted her, and not just to warm his bed.

But she was an enigma. He ran his fingers through his hair. Why did no one know her? Where was her family? Didn't anyone miss her?

He pulled out his ledgers, ready to work. Before Amelia he couldn't concentrate on his work because of an odd lack of interest. Now he couldn't concentrate because Miss Amelia Pence had taken over his thoughts. Hell, she'd taken over his entire being.

She arrived while he was at last busy at work.

"What can I do to help?" She stood in front of his desk, her bright smile in place, and all he wanted to do was push the papers onto the floor and pull her across the desk.

He sat back, putting at least some distance between them. "Before we begin, I feel as though I should apologize for last night. I make it a point to not dally with my employees. Ever. And I should not have kissed you last night. I can assure you it will not happen again."

Luckily, she did not mention that last night was not the first time he kissed her. Instead, she smiled and sat in the chair in front of his desk. "You are an honorable man, Mr. Rose. I can assure you I do not feel the need for an apology. If we were to be honest, I was as much involved in our encounter as you were."

Whatever did that mean? That she approved of what he'd done? He decided to try once more. He stood and walked around the desk. He rested his hip on the edge of the desk in front of her, and took her hand, linking their fingers together. "Can you please tell me what or who you are running from? There is no point in denying it because it's clear you are a lady, raised to have the sort of life most ladies of Quality have. Yet here you are working in a gaming club."

She gave a soft sigh. "I do not think you a stupid man. Of course, I realize you know there is something I am keeping from you, but for now I am not comfortable discussing it. Can you just accept that I am an employee of The Rose Room, and just want to do the best job I can?"

No, he did not want to accept that for several reasons, but she was leaving him no choice. He wanted her nearby. He wanted to protect her from whatever it was she was dealing with. He wanted to court her in a proper, acceptable manner. Above board, in public, not hidden in the shadows of the club. He might even want to take her to various *ton* events. Hold her in his arms as they danced, stroll in a darkened garden with her, or one of the paths at the Vauxhall Pleasure Gardens. All the things he'd eschewed for the last several years.

He looked down at their joined hands. As much as he hated having no control, and with everything inside of him chaffing at her request, if he wanted her, he would have to proceed on her terms. He glanced up at her bright blue eyes and smiled. "Let's get to work, then."

---

*A*melia glanced at the clock once again. Only three minutes had passed since the last time she checked. It was nearing nine o'clock, the time she would go down to the game floor and begin working.

She paced as she waited for Driscoll to arrive. He wanted to bring her down, introduce her to those employees she had not yet met, and then have her deal a couple of hands before they officially opened the doors at nine-thirty.

A quick glimpse at the mirror over the dressing table caused her to pause and assess herself. She was dressed in a dark red satin gown, snug over her belly and pulled into the back into a slight bustle. Black lace covered the center of the bodice all the way to the hem. The neckline was proper enough, and the slightly puffed short sleeves were trimmed with the same black lace.

The frock had recently been made by the dressmaker who had arrived at her room the week before to measure her. Driscoll had insisted that the new dresses she'd bought on her shopping trip with him would not do for her to wear while working.

He pointed out that all the men wore formal

evening attire, and she should as well. This gown was stunning, nothing like she'd ever owned. She would have felt more properly dressed had she been able to wear long gloves, but since she needed to use her hands to deal cards, she'd been given elbow length black lace gloves with the fingertips open.

Driscoll had sent Margie up to help her dress and do her hair. She was still embarrassed over the special treatment she was receiving, but he rightly pointed out that as the only female employee on the game room floor, she was setting a precedent.

Margie had parted her hair in the center, then softly pulled the mass of curls back, fixing it into a loose, but well anchored chignon at the crown, with a wisp of loose curls dangling from her temples.

She wore no jewelry, since she owned none, except the lovely strand of pearls her stepfather had given her when she turned eighteen. They'd been confiscated by Randolph when she arrived in London and most likely sold by now.

A slight knock on the door interrupted her musings. Taking a deep breath, she walked across the room and opened the door. Driscoll stood on the other side offering an encouraging smile. Since he was to spend time on the game room floor tonight, he was also dressed in formal evening attire.

He looked stunning. A curl from his dark hair fell on his forehead, giving him a rakish look. A well-cut black formal suit fit him perfectly, outlining his masculine form. He wore a silver and white waistcoat, with a black silk ascot tied smartly at his throat.

Her mouth dried up and her breathing hitched.

"You look beautiful, Amelia." He bent over her hand as if they were leaving for a social event. Suddenly she felt a stab of self-pity. She was raised to have a gentleman caller escorting her to balls, musicales, dinners and such. Not to escort her to a gaming club floor to work as a dealer.

She was mortified to feel tears gathering in her eyes.

Driscoll took her hand in his. "What is wrong, Amelia? Are you still nervous?"

His concern only made her feel worse. Before she knew it, tears streamed down her face and she turned from Driscoll trying her best to gain control.

"Amelia?" His soft voice broke through her sadness.

She turned back, swallowing several times, and placed a bright smile on her face. "I'm fine. Probably just nerves." Hopefully her shaky voice would convince him.

Driscoll studied her, the doubt in her remarks apparent on his face. But he did not push her, nor offer any additional kind words which would have sent her back to crying again. Instead, he withdrew a white handkerchief from his pocket and handed it to her.

She wiped her eyes and blew her nose, crumpling the handkerchief into a ball so she could wash it later. Raising her chin, she said, "I am ready."

He opened his mouth as if to say something, but instead nodded and waved her toward the door.

They walked side-by-side down the corridor to the stairs leading to the gaming floor.

The room was bustling. A man in the corner was setting up liquor bottles on a long table in front of him. He stacked clean glasses alongside the bottles. Other employees were cleaning, dusting and preparing the gaming tables. Driscoll took the time to introduce her to the employees she did not yet know.

"I think it might relax you a bit to play a couple of hands before we open the doors."

She nodded and a thought slammed into her that almost had her panicking. "My mask!"

"Ah, yes. I forgot. Wait here for me and I will fetch it from the office."

Amelia picked up the two decks of cards with shaky hands. She started to shuffle them when a man's voice called out, "Stop."

She froze and looked over at the man who had just been introduced to her as Mr. Maxwell Granger, who ran the hazard table. He moved from around the table and approached her.

"What?"

"It's best if you shuffle the cards in front of the players. They like to see that nothing untoward is going on."

"Oh, yes, of course. I'm sorry. I forgot."

"No need to apologize, young lady. I know this is all new to you." He leaned in and winked at her. "Remember, we were all new at one time."

She smiled back, the corner of her eye-catching Driscoll heading toward her, frowning at Mr. Granger.

"Best get that table set up, Granger." Driscoll's voice was anything but warm and friendly. Did he not like the man?

Mr. Granger merely offered Driscoll a smirk which Amelia did not understand at all. But she was distracted by the mask in Driscoll's hand. It was a beautiful black satin mask, the edges lined with black feathers. Small shiny stones were scattered throughout the piece.

Amelia let out a sigh of relief. The mask would cover almost half her face. All that would be visible was her mouth and chin. Since almost no one in London knew her, the only person she was concerned about recognizing her was Mr. Lyons, since she knew he was still a member in good standing at the club.

Even he, however, had not seen her in a clear light, so all he would remember of her was her hair color and height.

She slipped the mask on and turned to Driscoll. "Do I look mysterious enough?"

He grinned and her heart took a leap. "Yes, my

dear. Very mysterious." He leaned in closer. "And lovely. It will be no burden to stand near your table tonight."

Thankfully the mask hid most of the blush that rose to her face.

"Mr. Granger told me not to shuffle the cards until the players are seated."

"Yes. He is correct. I should have told you that. It makes the players feel like everything is above board if they can see that. Which, by the way, is the rule here. We don't cheat in any way, and we do not permit players to cheat either. If someone is caught cheating, he is banned from the club."

Amelia nodded, still mesmerized at how Driscoll looked in his formal clothes. Would he try to kiss her again tonight? A fluttering started in her stomach when she thought about it.

Now with him standing so close and the fragrance of his bath soap drifting toward her, she had the urge to throw herself into his arms and inhale his scent, feel his strong arms around her, taste his lips again.

Driscoll waved over two other staff members whose duties were done. Mr. Donald Johnson and Mr. Arthur Richards had been introduced to her earlier and both men seemed to be friendly enough. Mr. Johnson was in security and Mr. Richards was a 'runner'. He kept the guests happy by seeing that they had drinks and food if they desired and took care of submitting IOUs to the banker.

Mr. John Melrose ran the bank. He accepted the winnings from the tables, recounted the money turned in by each dealer, recorded it against each employee, then placed it into a safe after giving Driscoll the tally for the evening.

From what Amelia saw, The Rose Room was a very well-run, honest establishment. The brothers had done quite well for themselves.

The three men sat in front of her, and with a nod from Driscoll, she shuffled the cards and began to deal.

Despite her nervousness, she did quite well and did not fumble at all during the half hour they played. When the last hand finished, Driscoll leaned back in his chair and regarded her. "You are going to be quite a hit, Miss Pence."

Mr. Richards grinned. "I agree. Beautiful, smart, and competent." He looked at Driscoll. "You brothers have all the luck."

It wasn't Mr. Richards' words that had her blushing. It was the look Driscoll cast in her direction. Hunger, desire, and pride.

"Doors open," someone called from the front of the room. Mr. Johnson and Mr. Richards left her table with encouraging words as several men entered the room.

"I will be against the wall over there," Driscoll said as he stood. "If you need anything, anything at all, just nod in my direction."

Amelia touched her mask to make sure it was in place and took a deep breath. For reassurance, she looked over at Driscoll who smiled and winked at her.

In less than five minutes she had a full table. Obviously, the only woman in the room was a draw. She started out shaky, but soon got into the game and after a while was actually enjoying herself.

"Why would a beautiful woman like you work in a gaming club?" The man who had occupied her table for over an hour leered at her. He'd been commenting since he'd sat down and had refused to give up his seat to the many requests from the men waiting for a place behind the players.

He'd also had the runner bring him drinks at a steady pace, and his playing had gotten sloppy as he continued to imbibe.

She didn't stop her dealing but shrugged. "It's a job."

"I could think of another job I could offer you that

wouldn't require you being on your feet all night." Another player chimed in, nudging the man who asked the question.

"That's right. Better to be on your back, eh?"

"Gentlemen, I believe it's time to surrender your seats to other players." Driscoll had appeared out of nowhere, his hands on the shoulders of the two men who had been speaking with her.

The first man looked over his shoulder at Driscoll. "What? We're just having a little fun with the chit."

Driscoll placed his hands on the elbows of the two men and moved them up. "Time to go lads."

The second man tried to wiggle his elbow from Driscoll's grip. "Now wait a minute. I want to stay here."

Driscoll nodded in the direction of the hazard table and a man walked briskly to Amelia's table. She remembered him from the introductions. His name was Mr. David Sanders, one of the security guards.

"Let's go gentlemen." Mr. Sanders was a bit more forceful, and the two men stood, one of them stumbling as they were escorted from her table.

Amelia took a deep breath as a man and woman slid into their seats.

"Are you all right?" Driscoll moved behind her table and leaned close to her ear.

"Yes. I am fine."

He touched her arm. "I can have another staff member take over the table and give you a break whenever you need one."

She really loved his concern but didn't want to appear unable to work an entire shift. "Maybe later."

Driscoll studied her for a minute, then nodded and stepped away.

By the time another hour passed, Amelia's head was pounding, and her feet hurt like the devil. She'd avoided several requests to remove her mask and more than one suggestion that she consider another line of work. One on her back.

Driscoll never strayed far from her table which concerned her since she knew he generally spent most of the time the club was open upstairs working on his ledgers.

Eventually, about one thirty in the morning, Driscoll approached her with another man she'd been introduced to as Mr. Jason Fletcher. "Miss Pence, Mr. Fletcher will replace you for the rest of the night."

She shook her head, even though her headache had gotten worse. "No. I'm fine."

Driscoll ignored her and took her elbow to walk her away while Mr. Fletcher stepped in and began dealing, with grumbling from the men at the table at the loss of the female dealer.

"You're exhausted," he said as he marched her across the room and up the stairs.

"You don't understand, I have to do this. I need a job." She tried to pull her elbow away, but his grip was much stronger than she would have expected.

"No one is firing you, so calm down." He handed her another handkerchief when the tears began to fall again, gathering under her mask.

Amelia was so disappointed in herself, and thought she was much stronger than this. True, she had never held a job in her life, but she was certainly not a weak person.

They entered the dining room and Driscoll pulled out a chair for her. He sat alongside her and took her hand in his. "I assume you have never worked before, am I correct?"

Amelia sniffed and nodded.

"It will take some getting used to. Standing on your feet, constantly dealing cards, and thinking about what you are doing. It's tiring, but especially for someone who is not used to working."

Driscoll reached out and removed her mask, laying it on the table. Amelia took a deep breath, not realizing how constricting the mask had been.

The look in his eyes as he studied her would probably have frightened her if she weren't so blasted tired.

His fingers ran down her cheek with a very light touch. "I'm also not happy with the comments and suggestions tossed your way tonight." He stood and walked to the sideboard, leaning against it and crossing his arms. "This is not the place or the job for a lady."

Her eyes grew wide. "Please don't fire me. I know I can do this. I just need to get used to it all."

He rubbed his forehead with his index finger and thumb. "I am not firing you, Amelia. That is the last thing on my mind." He reached out and took her hand. "Come, I will escort you to your bedroom and we will talk tomorrow."

She took his hand and stood but didn't move. "I know you wasted your time tonight watching me, and your work has piled up. At least let me help you with that. It would make me feel better."

Driscoll cupped her face in his large hands, grazing softly over her cheeks with his thumbs. "Watching you is never a waste of time." Slowly he bent his head and kissed her. Lightly at first, then when she moved closer and leaned into him, her breasts crushed against his hard chest, he wrapped her in his warm, strong arms, and took the kiss deeper.

If only she could be sure he wouldn't turn her over to her stepbrother, she would tell him everything. Maybe this attraction between them would turn into something more. But she couldn't take the chance just yet. Men were still the ones in charge. They made all the decisions, and since Driscoll was a man of honor, he might very well think returning her to Randolph was the noble thing to do.

In other words, she was yet unable to trust him.

## 12

*D*riscoll tapped his pen on the desk and stared at the ridiculous painting of two love birds that Dante had received from one of his paramours and insisted on hanging on their office wall. Not that it mattered because Driscoll's eyes didn't really see it since his thoughts were miles from where he sat.

He was getting into trouble.

His feelings for the mysterious lady only a few doors down from his office were becoming complicated. Yes, he'd felt lust for her from the time she climbed to her feet after falling through the window. The rain-soaked shirt and trousers she wore highlighted every single curve the woman possessed. A man would have had to be dead not to react to that.

But now other feelings had given rise without him even aware of whence they arrived. Sneaking up on him, they did.

Protectiveness, caring, respect, curiosity, but most of all a desire to solve whatever issue it was with which Amelia was dealing. To be the knight in shining armor to her lady in distress.

She didn't belong on a gaming room floor dealing cards to men who made lewd suggestions and tossed out coarse invitations. She deserved marriage to a husband who adored her, provided for her, and protected her from lecherous men.

Children. Most of all, her caring and sunny nature would make her a wonderful mother.

He'd been quite cynical when his brother, Hunt, had announced he was marrying Lady Diana, also known as Lady Trouble. The woman had been a plague on Hunt's existence most of his life. Yet, all Hunt's convoluted feelings had eventually melded into love. Strong love. Protective love. About-to-have-a-baby love.

Truthfully, Driscoll had never given a great deal of thought about marriage for himself. His brother, the heir, was healthy and strong so Driscoll had never worried about the burden of inheriting. And now with Diana and Hunt's baby due sometime soon, Driscoll would thankfully move farther down the line.

With no need for the confining state of matrimony, he'd pushed it to the back of his mind, thinking some-day, when he had the time, he might look for a wife. Dip his toes, as it were, into the Marriage Mart. He'd select someone he could stand to look at over the breakfast table for the rest of his life and who would not make it a chore to bed her. A woman who was beyond the years of most debutantes, past the giggling and blushing stage.

He'd imagined a warm friendship between them, with caring and affection on both sides, but certainly not an encompassing love. From what he'd seen, love wasn't the primary reason people—especially of his class—married.

He told himself Hunt and Diana were the exception.

Since he and Dante had been building their business and watching their money grow, all his time and energy had been spent thusly. Hell, Driscoll didn't even live in a respectable house. He rented a flat not far from the club, always assuming one day he would look for a proper residence to either lease or purchase. Just like one day he would look for a wife.

Then a thought slammed into him like a fist to the gut. Perhaps 'one day' had crept closer to him when he wasn't watching.

The door to the office swinging open interrupted his meandering. Dante entered and collapsed into the chair in front of Driscoll's desk. He tugged at his cravat and yanked it off. "I'm glad the night's over. We had a much larger crowd than normal. Do you suppose word of a female dealer had spread?"

"Perhaps. Amelia's table was full the entire time she worked. Most times the table was three deep with men waiting to take a seat."

Dante stretched with a loud yawn and then rested his linked fingers on his middle. "How did she do? I saw you replace her a couple of hours ago."

"She did quite well, actually. No missteps that I could see. However—" He stopped, not exactly sure what he wanted to say.

"What?"

"I'm not sure we're doing her a service, Dante. Amelia should not be working in a gaming club." He leaned forward, resting his forearms on the desk. "She was insulted, propositioned, and spoken to as no lady should be."

"You don't know she's a lady, brother. In fact, we know nothing about her. If you're that concerned, and want to keep her on the payroll, put her in the kitchen, or add to our maid count. We can find someone to take her place at the table."

Driscoll sat back and shook his head. "I can no more abide putting a lady to work in the kitchen, or cleaning water closets than dealing cards to rakes and libertines."

Dante shrugged. "Then marry the chit."

The words Driscoll was about to speak came to a grinding halt.

*Marry her?*

Not realizing how his brother's easily tossed out words had affected him, Dante continued. "She's given you no choice. If she has family out there," he waved in the general direction of the window, "she doesn't want to accept whatever help they can give her. If she has no family, then this job is her means of support."

Completely ignoring Dante's suggestion that he could marry her, Driscoll said, "She can marry."

"Who? If not you, then one of the cads propositioning her? I would think they are more interested in making her their mistress."

Driscoll slammed his hand down on the desk. "I would never allow that!"

Dante stared at him, then offered a slight, knowing smile. "Sorry to gainsay you, brother, but you are in no position to decide what happens to Amelia. You are not her father, brother, or guardian." He smirked. "Or husband."

He rubbed his eyes, ignoring his last remark. "I know. But someone has to look out for her."

"So, Saint Driscoll steps up?"

"Enough." Driscoll stood. "I'm for a drink right now and then home to bed."

The brothers left the office together and took the stairs to the gaming floor.

Driscoll handed Dante a snifter of brandy. "Are you headed home? Or to Mrs. Bancroft's?"

"I should head home, but . . ."

They drank in silence and then departed. They took their separate carriages, Driscoll brooding the entire way home. He stepped out of the vehicle and looked up at the building where his flat was located. He shook his head as he climbed the steps. He really should think more on finding a decent house. Something in Mayfair, or Baker Street, maybe Portman Square.

Perhaps that had something to do with his ennui

lately. A sense of not moving forward. Was it truly time to give marriage a serious thought? A more respectable house and neighborhood? Set up his nursery?

The idea of attending the Marriage Mart events to find a bride never appealed to him. So many young, giggling girls and their ferocious mamas.

Maybe the right woman was not rushing from event to event looking for a husband. Perhaps as he'd noted previously, and as Dante had so casually mentioned, the true woman—for him—was right under his nose.

He smiled.

\* \* \*

"There's no getting away from it, Newton, you have to start attending these fancy *ton* balls and find your sister. I'm losing my patience." Daniel Lyons took another sip of brandy and stared bleary-eyed at his drinking partner.

Randolph waved his hand, almost knocking over the bottle of brandy that sat between them. "I doubt I would be accepted at any respectable event. And I haven't attended one in months. Years, maybe. Not really sure."

"Nonsense. You are a viscount; you will be welcomed at any fancy affair. Especially with all the desperate mamas looking for husbands for their darling daughters. I hear there are dozens of wealthy girls from America anxious to marry a title. At least you're young and passable in looks. More than most others who are hoping to save their hides by marrying money."

Randolph burped. "I'm not that far down that I need to sell my title to some American chit with beady eyes and a large nose. Anyway, I don't know why you think Amelia would be at any of those things. I've told you dozens of times, the girl doesn't know anyone in London."

Lyons slammed his glass down, sloshing liquid onto the table. "Bloody hell, man, she knows *someone*. She had no money to go anywhere else." He narrowed his eyes at his friend. "Unless you're lying to me about the blasted girl disappearing and don't want to make good on your bet."

Randolph's jaw dropped. "How dare you accuse me of being dishonorable! I would never renege on a bet."

"Dishonorable enough to sell your sister into prostitution." Malcolm Pringle, up to now the silent member of their little imbibing group lazily slouched in comfortable chairs in White's, spoke up. "Not well done, Newton. She *is* your stepsister."

"Mind your business, Pringle. This doesn't involve you," Lyons snapped.

Pringle shrugged. "Just saying."

"Well, say it to yourself. The chit is under Newton's control. He can do with her what he wants."

"Sad life women have." Pringle stretched out his long legs and crossed his ankles. "Doesn't seem right that she can be bartered away like a horse. Or slave."

For a fleeting second Randolph felt an embarrassed twist in his stomach. Then he pushed the thought away to dwell on something else. Maybe he *should* attend some of these *ton* events. He doubted Amelia would be at one, but perhaps he could find himself a wealthy wife. Like Lyons said, he had a title, and never had a problem attracting the ladies.

Of course, he'd never before tried attracting one of the respectable ones. But he could always try.

"Lady Broomfield is holding some sort of ball next week. I'm sure there's an invitation in the pile most likely sitting on your desk at home," Pringle said, reminding Randolph of the stack that he almost never went through. Warm lemonade, giggling debutantes and marriage-minded mamas bored him to tears. The girls were so well guarded a man was lucky to even get a kiss.

Randolph stretched. "I just might do that." He grinned at Lyons. "Maybe I'll find a rich wife and then I can pay you off and forget about Amelia."

Lyons shook his head and glared at him, his snifter of brandy halfway to his mouth. "No deal. I want the girl."

"You said you would take payment if she didn't turn up."

Daniel shrugged. "I've changed my mind. I want Amelia, and I want her soon. I don't care what you have to do. Just find her." He rose and left the club, swaying on his feet, not looking back.

"What are you going to do now, Newton?" Pringle asked.

"Find the bitch." He gulped the rest of his drink.

* * *

AMELIA TOOK one last look in the mirror to admire herself. The ringlets framing her face gave her an impish look. The new pale green linen dress, one of the several she'd purchased while on her shopping trip with Driscoll fit her well. The white embroidery on the cuffs of the sleeves and the bottom of the dress made it look like the perfect morning dress a young lady of Quality would wear.

And despite her current circumstances, she must remember that she *was* a lady of Quality. She'd been born that way, raised that way, and would one day return to that status.

She hoped.

Although it wasn't promising. With no family to speak of, no friends in London in the upper crust, it would be quite the challenge to find an acceptable husband. She could most likely secure a position as a companion to an older lady, or a governess to a lord's children. That would certainly be a proper position for her, but a suitable match would be almost impossible from there.

The fairy tales and the romance novels of Miss Austen and the Bronte sisters, where all works out well in the end for the poor heroine, were fiction. Amelia had to deal with real life. Her original plan to save enough money to move elsewhere was still foremost in her mind. Hopefully in her new location—maybe a cozy little village—she might attract a vicar or kindly shop owner. She didn't need a wealthy or titled husband. Just someone she cared for and who cared for her. A home of her own. Children to love and nurture.

All of those dreams were, unfortunately, dependent on not being forced to comply with Randolph's intentions. She shuddered remembering how close she'd come to being passed off as a mistress.

She left her bedchamber and made her way to the dining room, which was empty. Generally, Driscoll and Dante were present having their breakfast. But food sat in covered dishes on the sideboard, as well as pots of tea and coffee, so she assumed they would join her shortly.

She fixed her tea and took a seat, inhaling the satisfying aroma, the steam from the cup misting her face. She missed this one little indulgence when she'd been forced to leave her country home to live in London.

Randolph had refused to allow Cook to buy tea since his preference was coffee on his rare visits, but Cook had kept her own supply of tea and offered a cup to Amelia on occasion. Too embarrassed to let the lovely women know she had no funds with which to purchase her own tea, she accepted the treat without comment.

"Good morning, Amelia." Driscoll entered the room. "You are looking lovely today."

She felt the blush rise from her middle. "Thank you."

He went directly to the sideboard and filled his plate. "Aren't you eating?" He nodded at her empty place while he settled in his seat across from her and shook out his napkin, placing it on his lap.

"Not yet. I'm enjoying my tea first."

A slight sense of unease settled over her. As much as she'd enjoyed the kisses they'd shared, she was still troubled, hoping that Driscoll did not think her an easy woman who gave her favors to any man.

Driscoll, on the other hand, seemed quite cheerful and not at all concerned. But then, she was quite sure he'd kissed plenty of women, while his was her first kiss.

Dante strode into the room, a glower on his handsome face.

"What's wrong, brother? I expected you to be in the best of moods," Driscoll said. "Or didn't you spend the night—" He glanced over at Amelia and added, "Never mind. We'll talk later."

Once Dante was settled with a cup of coffee in front of him, Amelia stood and moved to the sideboard to fill a plate. She could hear mumbling behind her between the two brothers, but they spoke low enough that she could not make out the words. All she could tell was Dante was angry.

She joined them and almost groaned when she took her first bite of the fresh bread.

"Amelia, I did some work on the books last night and it looks like your table did outstandingly well." Driscoll smiled at her, almost like a proud parent, and again she blushed.

"Congratulations," Dante offered.

"But I didn't work the entire time."

Driscoll laughed. "That's the amazing part. The table returns dropped once you left the table."

Amelia smiled. "I guess I did all right."

Driscoll covered her hand with his and regarded her with a look that had her heart thumping and her insides fluttering. "Yes. You did."

They smiled at each other.

"Enough for me." Dante rolled his eyes and stood. "I have work to do." Coffee cup in hand, he left the room.

Speaking of work reminded Amelia of her promise. "I plan to help you with the books today. I know watching me last night took you away from your work."

Instead of arguing with her as she thought he would do, he said, "I would appreciate that."

When she flushed and studied her lap, he said, "Amelia, look at me."

She glanced up, sure that her face was red as a ripe apple. "What?"

"Please don't be embarrassed with me. I liked kissing you and I hope you enjoyed it, too."

She shrugged and drew circles on the table. "It was nice."

"Just nice?" He studied her, his deep brown eyes boring into hers. "I guess the next time I shall have to do better."

Amelia gulped the last of her tea and stood. "I will see you in the office."

*Next time?*

*hree weeks later*
"We have a problem, brother." Dante strolled into the office, pulled out the chair in front of Driscoll's desk and threw himself into it, his long legs stretched out, his feet crossed at the ankles. Although he appeared relaxed, the tension in his brother's body was palpable.

Driscoll's muscles tightened. He had a good idea what problem Dante referred to and he wasn't yet ready to discuss it. It had kept him awake the past two nights.

Feigning ignorance was his choice of reaction. "And what is that?"

Dante studied him for a minute. "I think you already know."

Driscoll pulled his spectacles off and rubbed his bleary eyes. He'd been going over the receipts for the past three weeks and no matter how many times he added and re-added, the answers were always the same.

"If you're referring to the drop in house receipts, I am aware of it."

Dante straightened and leaned forward. "Not the house receipts, Driscoll. Specifically, Amelia's table receipts. They were quite robust her first ten days, but the past week and a half they've slipped considerably. Every night."

That very point had been bugging Driscoll for days. "I am aware of that. However, it's quite possible the novelty of having a woman dealer has worn off and things have settled down."

"Good try." Dante grinned, despite his obvious annoyance. "I realize you haven't been watching her table as closely since you've had words with the few men who had been harassing her, but from what I've seen her table has been just as popular this past week and a half as it had been her first ten days. The only difference is now she is counting her money and turning it in herself instead of you helping her with it."

When Driscoll didn't comment, Dante continued, his voice lowered. "We have to once again consider that Amelia arrived here with nothing more than the clothes on her back, with no apparent home or relatives searching for her."

Driscoll cleaned his spectacles and put them back on. "I know all of that. But I sincerely believe she is not stealing from us. She has been nothing but pleasant, hard-working, and grateful for the help we've provided her."

Dante jumped up from his seat. "She could also be a former member of a well-trained cast on Drury Lane and a fine actress."

"Are you suggesting everything we've seen of Amelia in the past month has been a lie?" The amount of anger he felt at Dante's criticism startled him.

Running his fingers through his hair, Dante paced the room. "I don't know. I have to agree that aside from this missing money, she has not shown any indication of nefarious intentions."

Driscoll reflected on the problem as his brother continued to pace. If only he could convince Amelia to trust him with her secrets. Holding back as she was only made the drop in her receipts suspect.

He'd gotten very close to her in the past few weeks and was rather enjoying the feeling. They'd spent time together at the end of each shift, and they'd taken a few trips to Bond Street for shopping. He loved the enjoyment on her face when she remarked about how proud she was to be purchasing things with money she'd earned herself.

Also, in the past two weeks their kisses had become more daring each time they were alone together. They could not seem to keep their hands off each other. He spent almost as much time thinking about Amelia as he did working on his books, which had consumed his life for years.

He knew in his heart that had she arrived in his life during a normal course of events, he would probably have proposed marriage to her by now. She was sweet, caring, smart, beautiful, and kind. She would be a wonderful wife and excellent mother. Even the rest of the staff loved her, despite the additional benefits she received.

His feelings for her went deep, but always the niggle of doubt at the secrets she guarded so closely kept him on edge. Now the missing money only gave his already skeptical brother more reason to second guess their employee's background and intentions.

"I will speak with her. I think the questions will go easier on her if I am the inquisitor." Driscoll winced at the term. But sitting down with her, boss to employee, to inquire about things that would embarrass them both did indeed make him feel like an interrogator.

Dante headed to the door, obviously relieved to be done with his part in it. "Let me know what you uncover." He stepped out and came right back in. "I understand your reluctance to believe anything untoward about Amelia, but keep in mind we are running a business."

Driscoll nodded. "I understand."

He closed the books he'd been working on and headed down to the gaming floor. As usual, the room was packed; shouts of both distress and excitement rose above the crowd. He headed to Amelia's table which was full, and again a few men deep stood behind the players, awaiting seats.

A sense of pride rushed through him. She had come a long way from her first night. She dealt the cards efficiently and was able to count and keep track of each player's hands while bantering with the gamers.

Once Driscoll had made it known to the patrons that Amelia was there for the purpose of dealing cards and nothing else, and any lewd comments to her would result in the member being banned for a month, things had become much more pleasant at the vingt-et-un table.

And for Driscoll.

He had hated listening to the things said to her and came close to using his fists more than once. *Leave off and say no more, she is mine,* he screamed to himself more than once. The only quasi-negative thing that continued was the numerous requests from the players for her to remove her mask.

Amelia went from ignoring the appeals to flat out refusing with a curt answer. Unfortunately, it left the men placing bets on who the lovely new dealer at The Rose Room was. As far as he knew there were even bets recorded at White's and Brooks's gentlemen's clubs wagering books.

Driscoll took up his place along the wall so he could view Amelia's table clearly. All looked well, but it wasn't the playing that disturbed him, it was the money she counted and turned in each night.

Without mentioning why he wanted to know, he'd

questioned John, the banker who received the money after the club closed. To make it unknown to him who he was concerned about, he asked John to re-check all the receipts.

For three nights now John had assured him the amount of money each staff member turned in matched the numbers written, in their hand, on the paper that came with the muslin bag of money. Since John had been with them since they opened, he had no reason not to trust him.

On the other hand, he refused to believe his assessment of Amelia's character was so far off that she would steal from those who had aided her when she had nowhere to go.

As he studied her, he realized he could not be objective about this missing money situation. He would still question her, but he knew his heart wasn't in it.

It was otherwise engaged.

Unfortunately, with the woman who had dropped through his window on a rainy night a few weeks before giving no information about herself.

* * *

AMELIA SMILED as Driscoll sauntered around the room, glancing occasionally at her table. He looked quite dashing in his black trousers, silver threaded waistcoat and black jacket. His ascot, as usual, had been tied in a hurry.

He'd gone from watching her all night to only visiting once in a while. It made her feel good to know he believed her capable of handling the job. And truth be known, she looked forward to the tiny flutters that erupted in her stomach when she saw him coming down the stairs.

She was quite proud of how she'd learned to deal like a professional, and banter with the patrons. Most of all she loved being paid to do actual work. So many ladies—especially those of her class—never got the feeling of purchasing something with money they earned themselves. It was quite heady.

She'd grown comfortable and was even quite relaxed most of the night. One thing she'd been grateful for had been Driscoll putting a stop to the comments and offers for unsavory assignations from some of the men who visited her table.

However, she needed to stop seeing Driscoll as her savior, her knight in shining armor. Although they'd grown quite close, and she was thoroughly enjoying his kisses, touches and embraces, her initial plan had not changed.

For as comfortable as she had become, she could not be sequestered here for the rest of her life. Despite spending a bit of her pay on frivolous things for herself and repaying the Rose brothers for the items they had purchased for her when she first arrived, she was putting aside money to escape. Even though there had been no further talk about Randolph being allowed back into the club, she was still nervous that he would show up or Mr. Lyons would recognize her.

She'd almost had a fit of vapors when Lyons sat at her table a few nights before. He studied her for a while but didn't seem to know her. Of course, back when her brother's plan had been revealed to her, she'd questioned Randolph about why the man wanted her for his mistress since they'd never met. He told her Lyons had seen her from a distance one time when he was at the house for a party.

Only that one slight encounter combined with the mask, had apparently been enough to prevent him from shouting *Aha, I've caught you! You're mine. Bought and paid for.* And then dragging her from the place.

Could she trust Driscoll to stop that from happening?

Driscoll made some rounds of the other tables and when the night grew to a close, he came back to her. He leaned on her table and made light conversation as she counted her money, wrote the amount on the piece of paper and placed it all in the money bag. He escorted her to Mr. Melrose to hand over the bag and then they made their way upstairs.

It had become their habit to stop in the dining room and have a drink before he departed for the night for his own home.

"Are you happy here, Amelia?" Driscoll asked as he placed a glass of sherry in front of her. He took the seat across from her and sipped his brandy.

"Yes." She frowned. "Why do you ask?"

"Just ensuring all is well. You are a new employee, and we like to make sure none of the staff members have issues that we can help solve."

An alarm went off in her head. Was he thinking of firing her? Was *he* not happy with *her*?

"Is something wrong?" Her voice came out barely a whisper.

"Not at all," he responded. A bit too fast for her liking.

Perhaps it was time to address the one thing that did trouble her. "I still believe I should move my belongings downstairs with the other employees. I'm afraid talk will begin, if it hasn't already, about me living up here."

Anger flashed in his eyes. Unusual for Driscoll, always the calm and placid one compared to his edgy brother. "What sort of talk? By whom?"

She took a sip of the sweet sherry, avoiding a direct answer. "I don't want people to think that we are. . ."

His countenance softened and he leaned forward to run his finger down her soft cheek. "That we are what?"

"Um, you know." She could feel the heat rise in her face.

He stood and moved around the table, taking the

seat next to her. He pulled her to him, wrapping his arms around her middle, then tickling the tender skin under her ear. "No. I don't know. Tell me."

His breath was brandy-scented and warm, moist. She shivered and he placed soft kisses where his lips were. "That we are lovers?"

Amelia sucked in a breath. "Yes." Good lord, the way he said it had her wanting to drag him to her bedroom, remove all their clothes and find out just what happens when her body feels this sense of desperate need.

His teeth nipped at her earlobe. "Do you want to be?"

There went her idea that he was too much of a gentleman to ask such a thing.

He leaned back and regarded her. "Before you answer, please know that I have no intention of having an affair with you."

Her spirits dropped. Apparently, any attraction between the two of them was only in her imagination.

She stood. "Well, I am glad to hear that." Driscoll tugged at her hand as she began to walk away. "Wait."

She shook him off and made it as far as the threshold when he caught up to her. He linked their fingers together and stayed with her until she reached her bedroom door. "Good night, Mr. Rose."

The cad actually laughed. "Mr. Rose?" His long, slim fingers tangled in her hair, crushing the curls in his hand. "If we get that far, Miss Pence, far enough that we are sharing a bed, it would be with a permanent arrangement."

Before she could make sense out of what he said, he pulled her in for a kiss that had her knees buckling. He wrapped his arm around her waist and dragged her against his hard body. She gripped his shoulders as he swept into her mouth, tasting, nibbling, teasing.

Pulling back, he rested his forehead against hers, the air between them heavy with panting. "No privacy here." He reached for the latch and opened the door, drawing her inside.

He spun her around. She landed in his arms and he took possession of her mouth, her body—her very soul. Slowly his hand worked its way up between them to cover her breast. He rubbed his thumb over the nipple, bringing a low, soft moan from deep inside her.

"I want to pleasure you." He kissed her cheeks, eyelids, chin. "To hear you moan my name as you break apart in my arms." He scooped her up and carried her to her bed, laying her down, then after toeing off his boots, climbed in to stretch out alongside her. He cupped her chin, stroking her cheek with his warm fingers. "I promise I will not take your virginity. Not yet. But I want to give you a taste of what we can share together."

Still reeling from what had happened so far, she merely nodded, the blood pounding in her head.

Once again, he plundered her mouth as his hand worked its way under her skirts, up her leg, past her calf, above the ribbons holding up her stockings. She inhaled deeply when his fingers reached the soft curls at the juncture of her thighs. His thumb circled a part of her there that came alive.

She gasped. "Oh, my. That feels so good."

Driscoll gave her a slight, very male-satisfaction smile. "It gets better, sweetheart. Hold on."

He continued to plunder her mouth as his fingers played with her sex. She grew agitated, restless. She needed more. "I, I feel as if I need something, Driscoll."

"I know love, just lie back, let me do the work."

She had no idea what he meant; all she knew was she didn't want him to stop doing whatever it was he was doing to her body. To her soul. She thrust her hips forward, pushing her mound against his hand, searching, reaching. "Please."

"Shh, Amelia. Relax. Don't try so hard." He kissed

her, which distracted her very little from where his fingers were busy. Finally, she groaned and pulled him closer, holding him tight as the most wonderful feeling swept over her, coming in waves that she never wanted to end. Her lips were dry, her lungs gasping for air.

She collapsed back onto the bed, and slowly opened her eyes to see Driscoll staring at her with an expression on his face that terrified her.

*Oh dear, what have I done?*

## 14

"*I* found the bitch." Daniel Lyons dropped into the chair alongside Randolph at White's where he was enjoying a glass of brandy with Sir John Devlin.

"Amelia?" Randolph almost spewed out his brandy at Lyons' blasé announcement.

"The very one." Lyons signaled the footman to bring a drink.

Randolph was practically speechless. They'd spent weeks scouring London looking for his stepsister and here Daniel just casually drops the information. "Where?"

Lyons took a sip of his brandy and leaned back, a cat-who-stole-the-cream look on his face. "At the Rose Room."

"The gaming club?" Devlin asked.

"Yes. She's a dealer."

If Lyons had announced that Amelia was working as a whore in the stews at Seven Dials, he wouldn't have been more surprised. How the bloody hell did she end up in one of the most well-known gaming clubs in all of London?

He hadn't realized he'd mumbled it out loud until

Lyons said, "I have no idea, but there she was—wearing a mask I might add—and dealing at the vingt-et-un table."

Devlin looked between the two men. "What's this all about?"

Lyons gulped the last of the brandy from his snifter and waved at the footman for a refill. "Just leave the bottle," he said when the man arrived. Then he turned to Devlin. "Our friend here wagered his stepsister in a card game. He lost—" he grinned at Randolph, "and I won."

Devlin frowned. "Won in what way?"

Lyons grinned. "She's now my mistress."

"You have her?" Randolph finally found his voice after grasping Lyons's words. He pushed back on the slight feeling of guilt that crawled its way into his thoughts. Since he could no longer afford to keep the girl fed and clothed, and with her dowry long gone, she was better off with Lyons. At least he wasn't a mean man and would not require her to do things that would hurt her.

Lyons shook his head. "No. It wasn't possible for me to just lean across the table and grab her. I mean there must be some dignity to this whole thing. Besides, one of the Rose brothers had his eyes fixed on her almost all night."

Devlin looked back and forth between the two men and leaning back let out a low whistle. "Isn't there some sort of a law against that?"

Randolph drew himself up in indignation. "It was a wager between two gentlemen." Bugger it, why did the man have to even be here while they had this conversation? If Randolph intended to find himself a wealthy wife, it would not do to have this information bandied about.

"Between two gentlemen, you say? Clearly your

stepsister didn't agree, or she would not have disappeared."

Randolph gritted his teeth. Judgmental fool. "No matter. She will do as she is told. She has—or so I thought—no other choices. I have been providing for her since my father died, but with my own funds quite low, it was time for her to pay me back."

Having dismissed Sir John's disapproving stance, he turned to Lyons. "Since she's now turned up at The Rose Room, all we need do is snatch her one night when the place closes."

Lyons pulled out his pocket watch and stood. "Perhaps. Right now, I must be off. I have an appointment with my tailor. I will call on you later tonight, Newton to go over the plan to retrieve my goods."

Randolph winced at Lyons' choice of words but shook it off. He needed Amelia to settle this debt since he had no blunt to pay it himself.

Sir John watched Lyons leave, then turned to Randolph. "I say, Newton, while I certainly don't agree with what you and Lyons have cooked up, I'm surprised you would offer such a sweet morsel for a single gaming debt."

Randolph drew himself up. "Why not?"

"Thinking like the economist I am, it occurred to me you are paying one debt with the girl. If the chit is so desirable, I'm surprised you didn't set up an auction." He grinned and shook his head, taking another sip of brandy.

Randolph's jaw dropped. What a grand idea! "You mean, get a few gentlemen together, offer her to the highest bidder. That sort of thing? Have you been to one of those?"

It was Devlin's turn to look stunned. "I was joking, old man. I would never participate in such an event." He pointed at Randolph. "And you would be wise to take it as meant. A joke."

Randolph waved his hand in dismissal. "Of course, I was just playing with you." His mind in a whirl on how he could set something like that up, he finished his brandy and stood. "Well, I must be off. I have appointments myself."

He strode from the room, glancing around quickly to see who he thought might be interested in such an event. Miles Martin caught his eye. He'd just dismissed his mistress the week before. Then there was Lord Beltran who was always up for new flesh.

There were others who came to mind, those who enjoyed life to the fullest, living the life of sin and debauchery, who would certainly be interested. Smiling and mentally rubbing his hands, his heart pounding with excitement, he left the club. Yes, this was a fine idea.

Then he came to an abrupt halt, almost causing the couple behind him in front of a haberdashery to run into him. He apologized and crossed the street.

Once they snatched the girl Lyons was expecting to take her immediately. How the devil to deal with that issue? While he was busy compiling the list of gentlemen to invite to the event, he would have to figure out how to get out of his debt to Lyons. Without resorting to pistols at dawn. After all, he was a gentleman.

* * *

DANTE LEANED against the doorjamb to Driscoll's office, studying his brother. "What's the news, brother?"

Since there was no point in pretending he didn't know what Dante was implying, Driscoll leaned back and tapped his pencil on the desk in front of him. "Lower receipts again."

Dante continued to glare at him, almost to the point where Driscoll felt like shifting in his seat.

"We have to speak with the girl, Driscoll. We cannot continue as if nothing is wrong. Despite her active table her returns for the night have consistently been lower than her ten days when you were watching her."

Driscoll ran his fingers though his hair. "I know. But something tells me there is more than the obvious answer to the puzzle."

Dante snorted. "I know what the 'something' is that's keeping you blindfolded to the chit."

Driscoll gritted his teeth, his blood pumping furiously through his body. "Do. Not. Call. Her. That."

"Which one? Chit or thief?"

Within seconds Driscoll was across the room and had his brother by the throat on the floor. "Amelia is not a thief!" He drew his fist back and clipped him on the jaw.

They rolled around the floor throwing punches until the door to the office opened.

"Whatever is going on in here?" Amelia stood with her hands on her hips, glaring at the two of them. "I can't believe two grown men—brothers no less—are fighting like a couple of street urchins."

Driscoll shoved Dante away and stood, dusting off his jacket. Dante climbed to his feet, rubbing his chin. He pointed his finger at Driscoll. "Take care of it." He strode to the door, rearranging his clothes. He pulled the door open and turned back. "Or I will."

Amelia flinched when the door slammed, then walked to Driscoll and fussed with his jacket, fixing the collar while he stood staring at her. No matter what the evidence, and despite his fondness for her, he could not believe she would steal from them.

Before he could change his mind, he drew her closer, wrapping his arms around her shoulders and waist. Her hands stopped and rested on his chest. He lowered his head and captured her soft lips. He brushed his lips back and forth until she leaned into him with a slight moan.

All the passion mixed with fear from Dante's accusations turned the kiss into something more than he'd ever shared with her before. More than he'd ever shared with any other woman.

Amelia was his. He might have a small doubt in his mind due to his brother's accusations, but there was no question about his feelings, and his desire to take the next step.

He pulled back and smiled. Her eyes were glassy, her short breaths coming rapidly, drawing his eyes to her delectable breasts.

She drew small circles on his jacket with her fingertip. "What was that all about?"

Driscoll slid his palm down her arm and linked their fingers. "Let's take a walk to the dining room and have our nighttime drink."

* * *

AMELIA CONTINUED to stare at him, waiting for her question to be answered. When he moved forward and led her from the office to the dining room, she followed him.

She was beginning to believe she would follow Driscoll anywhere. Her feelings for the man had grown ever so much since she fell through his window. She enjoyed his kisses and caresses and wondered how it would feel to allow him further liberties. Although an innocent miss, she was not an ignorant one.

There was no doubt in her mind that Driscoll desired her, she felt the evidence of his hunger pressed up against her belly every time they embraced.

She also recognized the feelings that settled in her stomach when he was near. She shivered thinking about the time he pleasured her. Next time would he remove her clothes and run his large, warm hands over her naked skin, then take her to bed?

"Are you chilled, sweetheart?" He frowned and pulled out a chair for her to sit. When she nodded, he shrugged out of his jacket and placed it over her shoulders. She pulled the jacket closed and inhaled the smell of its owner. Male, spicy, warm. Driscoll.

Dare she tell him she shivered from anticipation? Would he then consider that statement as her consent and do what she'd been thinking about and dreaming about for weeks? To finish what they'd started the last time they were alone together?

Best to remove those thoughts from her mind. Although it was hard to keep herself focused on it, she hadn't altered her plans because of this attraction between them. Lately, despite the increase in Driscoll's attentions to her, she sensed a holding back that had not been there the first couple of weeks she'd worked for The Rose Room. There were times when he just studied her, a question he obviously wanted to ask, but refrained from doing so. Almost as if he didn't trust her.

Which was quite understandable since she did not trust him completely, or she would have shared her troubles with him by now. A bit of trust missing from both of them. For as far as they'd come it was doubtful they could go any further until they trusted each other.

"WELL, look who's still lollygagging at the breakfast table. Don't you have work to do?" The morning after their fistfight, Dante entered the breakfast room at Huntington Townhouse in Mayfair, Driscoll right behind him. "At least that's what you always tell me when I'm on a well-deserved break at the club."

Hunt grinned as his brothers pulled out chairs and

117

sat. Dante reached for a slice of toast and the jar of jam to top it with. He smiled at Hunt's wife, Diana, who was quite close to delivering their first baby. "How is my favorite sister-in-law feeling today?"

"Tired. Bored. Ready to have the baby." She smiled, the strain on her face and her pallor confirming her words.

After examining his wife carefully, Hunt turned to Dante. "I do have work, in fact. I have to check over the financial statements you sent me." He frowned at Dante. "What happened to your chin?"

Dante waved his hand. "I walked into a door."

Driscoll took an orange from the middle of the table and began to peel it. "Going over the statements. Don't trust your kin?"

Hunt grew serious. "I trust you, as you well know. But mistakes happen."

"Lately there seems to be a lot of mistakes coming from Miss Pence's table," Dante said and glanced over at Driscoll.

Driscoll cast his brother a warning glare. The last thing he wanted was to end up rolling about the floor again in front of his sister-in-law. "I'm sure everything is fine."

"*Miss* Pence? You have a woman working at The Rose Room?"

"Yes, and her table is swarmed every night," Dante said between bites. Hunt had generally appeared at the club a few times a week. However, as the arrival of the Huntington heir grew closer, Hunt had been absent more than present.

Hunt looked over at Driscoll. "Whatever made you hire a woman?"

"She's smart, talented, a good worker and the members love her." His words were clipped as if expecting Hunt to challenge him.

Hunt shrugged. "Your decision." He looked at Dante. "What is the problem with her table?"

"Nothing," Driscoll said as Dante also answered, "Shortages."

Diana rose, and all three brothers jumped to their feet. "Well, I will leave you gentlemen to fight this out. I am going to take a short lie-down before Hunt and I go for our ride this afternoon."

"Are you well, Diana? You look a little drawn." Hunt studied her as he rounded the table to take her arm.

"I'm fine. Just a bit tired, as I said. I also have been troubled by a backache all night."

"Should I send for Dr. Reading?" Hunt frowned as he led her out of the breakfast room, calling for her maid to assist her upstairs.

"No."

Driscoll lowered his voice. "I prefer not to bring this up here and now, Dante."

"Hunt is a partner, or have you forgotten that minor fact? He has as much right to know about shortages as we do."

"Not until we have done more research on it ourselves."

"Ah, but I feel as though you are not doing the proper research."

Driscoll placed his fisted hands on the table. "Exactly what is it you are accusing me of?"

"Are you two still arguing about Miss Pence?" Hunt took his seat and studied the two of them.

"There is nothing wrong with Miss Pence's final tally reports." Driscoll practically growled at Dante.

Dante shrugged. "If you say so."

"How did you find this female dealer?" Hunt motioned to the footman to bring another pot of coffee.

"She fell into his lap, as it were," Dante said, grinning widely.

Driscoll made to jump up and swing at his brother. Hunt grabbed the back of Driscoll's jacket. "Knock it off. What's the matter with the two of you? And don't think for one minute I believe you walked into a door, Dante. More like into Driscoll's fist."

"Hunt!"

The scream from upstairs had Hunt jumping up and racing to the breakfast room doorway. A woman, who Driscoll assumed was Diana's lady's maid met him, wringing her hands. "Her waters have broken, my lord."

"What? Did she spill a glass of water on herself? Is that why she's wailing up there?" He gestured with his thumb at the floor above them and the sound of Diana crying.

"No, my lord. Her waters have broken. You must send for Dr. Reading."

"Well, why didn't you say so, instead of talking about spilled water?" Hunt headed to the front door. "Peters, send for Dr. Reading. I think Lady Huntington is having the baby."

Dante and Driscoll looked at each other and immediately left the breakfast room. "I think this is a good time for us to take our leave." Driscoll pounded Hunt on his back. "Send word when it is all over."

Like two scurrying lads in trouble with the headmaster, Driscoll and his brother grabbed their hats from Peters and fled the house.

## 15

"*O*h, yes, Miss, the gowns and jewelry the ladies wear will make you swoon!" Margie's eyes grew wide as she described the upcoming ball to Amelia.

Margie, Amelia, Betsy, and even Mrs. Bannon, the cook, were sipping afternoon tea at the long worktable in the kitchen and raising each other's delight at the impending event.

"I am very excited. I've never been to a fashionable ball before," Amelia said. 'Twas quite unfortunately true, despite her birth. All she'd been able to attend were a few local assemblies while in residence at the Newton country estate. As the daughter of a marquess and stepdaughter of a viscount, she'd grown up dreaming of her own Season, visits to the modiste, rides in Hyde Park, suitors calling with flowers spouting poor poetry, musicales, the theater and museums. And most of all, dancing until dawn with handsome gentlemen.

Given her current circumstances, a fairy tale, to be sure.

"We have gowns in storage you can borrow," Betsy said, directing her comment to Amelia. "Most of us will do the same. Mr. Rose and his brother were kind enough when we held the first ball to make sure all the employees were included, and that they had appropriate clothing to wear."

Although she'd never worn other women's clothes before she came to The Rose Room, she was grateful to at least have something nice for the ball. As elegant as her work gowns were, they were just that. Work gowns. If she weren't saving every penny for her escape, she would buy something new, but since this life was not hers forever, she could not justify the waste of money.

"I say, 'tis only a week until the ball. Why don't we visit the storage room now and see what we have for Miss Pence?" Betsy stood abruptly, not waiting for anyone's agreement.

"Yes." Margie clapped her hands and looked over at Mrs. Bannon. "Do we have time before we need to prepare for tonight's supper?"

The older woman smiled at the young girls' enthusiasm. "Yes. I believe we do." She glanced at the clock on the counter against the wall. "We have about thirty or forty minutes."

They immediately vacated the kitchen and hurried down the hall to what Betsy pointed out was the storage room. Amelia could feel the excitement building as they opened a large wooden wardrobe and began pulling out gowns.

There were seven or eight garments of various colors. Most of them in more subdued shades. Although Amelia had always imagined her first ball dressed in something white, or a pale color, befitting a young, unmarried miss, she was more than happy to consider any one of these gowns.

She particularly liked a deep green satin gown. She held it up and looked in the mirror attached to the wardrobe door.

"That looks lovely on you, miss," Margie said. "You will be turning young men's heads all night."

Amelia doubted that very much. Although she hadn't spent time at fancy events, she knew the women who would attend the ball the following week would wear the height of fashion, in vivid colors, with jewels draping their necks, wrists and ears. Most likely purchased by their protectors.

But then again, her primary reason to attend the ball was to have fun. To finally experience what she'd dreamed about as a girl. To dance and possibly flirt, at least once before she left London to start her new life somewhere else.

"Here, Amelia, this mask appears to match that gown." Mrs. Bannon handed her a half face mask—quite similar to the one she wore each night—but in a color matching the gown.

"Yes, I believe you're right." Amelia held the mask up to her face.

"Are you taking that one, then?" Betsy asked.

Amelia moved back and forth in front of the mirror, holding the gown against her body. "Yes. I believe so." She looked at the other women. "Unless one of you wanted this one?"

Mrs. Bannon laughed—her larger size denying any intention she would have had regarding that gown. The other two women shook their heads. "I wore that one last year," Margie stated.

"'Tis not my color," Betsy added as she pulled out a bright yellow gown with feathers and lace at the neckline. Amelia tried very hard not to cringe.

She had some time before she needed to dress for the night and help with setting up the club, so she hurried with the gown flung over her arm to her room to try it on.

. . .

O<small>NCE SHE WAS</small> out of her plain day dress, she held up the gown and smiled. She could use a much sturdier corset. The one she wore when working was softer since she had to wear it for hours while standing on her feet. And it would be truly lovely to indulge in silk stockings.

She pulled the gown on anyway, just to see if it fit without the correct corset. After stepping into it and pulling it up to her shoulders, there was a slight knock on her door.

Holding the front of the gown against her chest with the entire back open, she walked to the door, noting the hem on the gown needed to be shortened. "Yes?"

"Amelia, it's Driscoll."

She opened the door to see him leaning his arm against the doorjamb. "Oh, sorry, I didn't know you were dressing." His eyes were fixated on the neckline of the gown, much lower than the ones she wore while dealing each night. Then he followed the line of the dress down to her toes. "It's too long." His voice was gravelly, and he swallowed a few times.

Amelia stepped back, her face flushing at the look in his eyes. "It's one of the gowns from the wardrobe in storage." She fumbled, trying to keep the dress from falling to the ground. "I had hoped to wear it to the ball next week."

Driscoll seemed to have lost his train of thought. He just stood there and gaped at her.

Amelia cleared her throat, the tension between them growing. "Do you need to talk to me?" She felt stupid. Of course, he needed to speak with her, why else would he be standing in her doorway?

"Um, yes." He raised his eyes to hers. The heat in his eyes frightened her, while at the same time feelings of warmth and an unnamed need filled her entire body, taking away her breath.

He shook himself and stepped back. "I will wait for you in the dining room, for when you are—" He waved in her direction, continued to back up until he hit the wall behind him, then quickly made his way down the corridor.

*  *  *

DRISCOLL COLLAPSED into the chair in the dining room and banged his fist on the table. What a complete arse he'd made of himself. Just because Amelia was standing there half-undressed with her hair down around her shoulders looking as if she just stepped from a well-used bed was no reason to behave like a green youth with his first woman.

He was an adult and had enough affairs under his belt to qualify as experienced. Yet something about Miss Amelia Pence reduced him to practically a blathering idiot.

He had finally worked up the nerve to confront her with the—assumed—missing money. He had no intention of accusing her, merely having a conversation about how she conducted her table, how she stored her money while dealing and filling out the receipt slip and placing it with all the money in the bag to give to John.

She'd been employed by The Rose Room for more than four weeks. The strong returns at the beginning had dwindled the last couple of weeks. No matter how hard he tried to deny it, he had to face the fact that money was missing. Without saying why to either man, he'd had one of the security guards and an assistant manager watching her table.

The reason he'd given them for the scrutiny was he wanted to avoid any harassment of the young lady. They had reported back to him all was well, she was doing a fine job, even in handling drunk men who made improper comments.

He was proud of her when he received those reports, but he still had to address the question of the missing money. He'd gone through his ledgers, back to when Marcus had the table. Amelia's returns had surpassed his for the first week and a half, then dropped below what he had turned in since then. Yet she was drawing a much larger crowd than Marcus ever had.

Driscoll stood as Amelia entered the room. She had changed into one of her day dresses and her hair was put up in a chignon at the top of her head. Gone was the flushed, just-left-the-bed look that had driven him into idiocy.

He pulled a chair out for her and she sat. She glanced over her shoulder and said, "Would you like a cup of tea? I think I will have one."

Happy to have anything to avoid the conversation he nodded, and she hopped up to pour. He rose and followed her, taking one of the cups from her hand. "Thank you."

They seated themselves again and Driscoll took a deep breath. "It's been nearly five weeks since you've been with us, Amelia. How are you faring?" He offered what he hoped was a sincere, friendly smile.

She blew on the liquid and took a sip. "Fine. I am quite happy with the job." She lowered her cup and frowned. "Is there a problem?"

Apparently his sincere, friendly smile hadn't worked. "No. No problem." He took a sip of tea. "Well, just a little one."

"What's that?"

He cleared his throat and sat back, again attempting the sincere, friendly smile. She looked more confused than nervous. Wasn't that proof that she hadn't done anything wrong? "It's not really a problem. I just wanted to tell you I will be gone for possibly a few weeks."

Her eyebrows rose. "Gone? Where?"

"This is confidential."

Amelia nodded.

"I take assignments on occasion for the Crown. I have been asked to help break a code that involves a great deal of numerical coding. Since I am fairly adept at numbers. . ."

Amelia grinned. "That's wonderful. Does everyone know you do this sort of thing?"

Driscoll shook his head. "Only my brothers."

"Why are you telling me?"

He shrugged. He didn't know why he was telling her, actually. It started as a way to avoid discussing the money situation. Then he realized he wanted her to know that about him. His thoughts ran more along a permanent arrangement between them in the future. Possibly the near future.

Nothing that Dante said would dissuade him from believing Amelia would not steal from them. He also hoped by telling her these little things about himself she might feel comfortable to open up and confide in him. Let him know what or who she was running from.

"When are you leaving?" She actually looked troubled as she gazed at him over her teacup, which gave him hope.

"First thing tomorrow morning."

"And you must stay there?"

He nodded. "Yes. Until the code is broken. There will be two others working with me."

She grinned. "Number geniuses, too?"

"Hopefully."

She avoided his eyes, her fingertip drawing small circles on the table. "Who will do your work while you're gone?"

"There are others who are familiar enough with the workings to at least do some of the work. The rest I will complete when I return." He reached out and tucked a loose curl behind her ear. "I've done this before."

"Um, is it dangerous?"

He laughed. "No. Not at all. Numbers don't generally attack you."

"Don't laugh," she huffed. I imagine this sort of assignment holds a certain amount of danger. Otherwise, you wouldn't be keeping it all a secret." A soft smile teased her lips. "I will miss you."

Dear God, that was the wrong thing to say. He covered her hand with his. "I will miss you, too."

As if a thought suddenly entered her mind, she looked up at him, wide-eyed. "You won't be here for the ball?"

Hating to disappoint her—and himself—since he was looking forward to holding her in his arms, he said, "No. Most likely not. Unless we get very lucky and break the code quickly."

"Do you think that will happen?"

He shrugged. "One never knows."

He glanced at his pocket watch. "It's time to prepare for the night." He pushed his chair out and stood. Amelia hopped up before he could assist her. She twisted her fingers and looked as though she wanted to say something, but then shook her head and left the room, taking her captivating scent with her.

It would be a long assignment this time.

* * *

"THERE's a ball the brothers have every year at the Rose Room. The masquerade where true ladies are even welcome. Most times there are hundreds of people in attendance. As an employee, Amelia will be there. All we have to do is get her alone, snatch her and we're done."

Randolph listened to Lyons who had come up with

the plan on how to get their hands on Amelia. He still hadn't told him he'd changed his mind about allowing him to take her for the gambling debt. It made much more sense to auction her off, take the profit, pay Lyons off and have some blunt left for himself.

"Yes. But you forget I have been banned by the bastards." Randolph started to laugh. "Do you understand? Bastards. Well, at least one of them is a bastard." He took another swallow of his brandy.

"Pay attention, Newton. This is our best opportunity to get the girl. You forget this is a masquerade ball. That means costumes. Masks. If you enter with me, no one will stop you. They are looser about who enters at this affair. You should know. You've gone to a few yourself."

Randolph nodded. He just wanted to get his stepsister under his control. He'd already secretly sent out word about the auction. Time was growing short because he wanted to build up interest, but he didn't want to have Lyons find out until they had her in hand. If he were to snatch her away from The Rose Room, he needed Lyons' help.

"Fine. When is this event?" Randolph asked.

"A week from Thursday."

"I'll be ready." Randolph downed his drink and waved to the footman for more. Soon he would have plenty of blunt to cover his bill here at White's and take care of his tailor and haberdasher who had begun to hound him. And had the nerve to make threats. To him, a peer!

What he needed was a wealthy wife to provide a robust dowry so he could live the life he deserved. The money from the auction would put him in a position to present himself at ton events properly dressed to capture a wealthy woman. From what he'd heard throngs of American heiresses were arriving in

London, their parents anxious for their little darlings to secure a title.

Well, he'd give them a title all right. He wasn't too proud to admit his title was for sale. He leaned back and sipped his drink. Yes, things were certainly looking up.

## 16

"Do you have any idea how long this assignment will take?" Dante sat on the floor, leaning against the wall in Driscoll's bedroom, swirling a snifter of brandy as his brother packed for his trip to an undisclosed site somewhere in England to work on the code he was expected to crack.

"Not long I hope," Driscoll said, stuffing a few more items into his bag.

"I don't suppose you addressed the issue of the missing money with Amelia?" He took another swallow watching his brother carefully over the rim of the glass.

"There wasn't time," he mumbled, hoping Dante would accept that answer. He snapped the satchel closed and turned to his brother. "Before I accuse an employee of stealing, I feel we need proof."

"What proof? The numbers tell the story. When Marcus had that table, the returns were better than Amelia's last few weeks." He pointed his finger at Driscoll. "If you intend to use the 'lack of experience' excuse, it won't work since as you know, the first ten days of her working that table, her returns were tremendous."

Driscoll pulled his spectacles off and rubbed his

eyes with his fists. "I don't want to discuss this right now. I want to get this assignment over with. Then I will address the problem with Amelia." When Dante opened his mouth to speak, he added, "That is the end of it for now, brother. I agree, something is going on, and I don't like losing money any more than you do. But I swear to you once I return, I will solve this mystery."

He picked up his bag and left his bedchamber. Dante followed him to the front door and outside to the waiting carriage.

Once Driscoll settled himself into the carriage, he reached out to close the door. "Please promise me you won't do anything rash until I return."

Dante's lips tightened and he shrugged. "I agree to wait." Switching from the touchy subject between the brothers, he said, "Is there danger involved in this assignment?"

Driscoll laughed. "Numbers? I doubt it." He closed the door and gave Dante a slight wave.

As they made their way through the crowded streets to an undisclosed location, Driscoll attempted to put Amelia and everything confusing about her from his mind. Since only the driver—sent by Sir Phillip, their contact at the Home Office—knew where they were headed, Driscoll had no idea how long the trip would take. They might even leave London.

He leaned his head back and tried his best to clear his mind. Cracking codes was not dangerous—as Dante had asked—but it did take full concentration on his part. The job would only take longer if he was unable to focus. He was anxious to get back to the club and put an end to these questions about Amelia.

It was during the trip that hadn't taken more than an hour that he decided to do exactly what he'd been dancing around for weeks. Once he returned, he would question Amelia about the money and about her background. In fact, he would demand answers. Their relationship had grown to where they had to trust each other or there would be no moving forward.

And moving forward is exactly what he planned to do.

* * *

THE NIGHT of the well-known Rose Room Autumn ball was the only day the famous gaming club removed the gaming tables and allowed dancing, drinking, and granted permission to proper ladies to attend the festivities. It had started as a way to build the membership a couple of months after the brothers had bought the business. It had been so successful that they continued it each year.

Paying for the liquor, decorations, music, food, and the lack of gambling did put a dent in the profits, but the return over the following weeks was significant each time they held the ball.

Amelia had learned all of this from her co-workers as they all helped set up the room to resemble a ballroom as fine as any prestigious house in London.

As much as she looked forward to the beautiful gown she was to wear, and the thought of actually attending a real ball, her spirits were dampened by Driscoll's absence.

She had foolishly hoped his assignment would end before the ball, but she'd heard nothing from him, and was not comfortable asking Dante about it because he seemed to withdraw from her more each day. His friendly, easy banter that she had enjoyed so much when she'd first been hired had changed to a more somber attitude when he was around her. Not sure what to make of that, she focused on her job and waiting for Driscoll's return.

Although she continued to add to her pile of coins

safely hidden in a box under her bed, truth be told she was no longer certain she would escape London when she had enough money. Her feelings for Driscoll had grown over time and now with his absence, she realized it would not be easy to walk away from The Rose Room. And him.

During his absence, she'd decided the time had arrived for her to trust him enough to tell him about Randolph and his plan for her. The obvious possessive mien on Driscoll's face when they were around other men had convinced her he would never allow her to be handed over to another man as his mistress.

Driscoll was an honorable man. Even though Randolph was legally her guardian, honorable men did not allow innocent, unprotected women to be wagered in a card game. Of that she was certain.

Now with the room set up, her part of the job was finished, and she was enjoying a bath in the bathing room and would soon dress in the lovely gown she'd gotten from the wardrobe. After taking up the hem and removing a few extra ruffles that she thought did nothing to enhance the garment, she carefully pressed it and it now hung in her room.

Margie, Betsy, Mrs. Bannon and Amelia were to meet in the kitchen before they dressed to fix each other's hair. Because until a couple of years ago Amelia had had her own maid, she wasn't exactly adept at fixing anything more intricate than a chignon. After the first time Betsy had fixed her hair, Amelia had taken over, not wanting to have Betsy believe that lady's maid to another employee had been added to her duties. But the ladies were so enthusiastic about the ball she didn't think her lack of abilities to help out would deter them from having a good time if their hair was simply styled.

In less than an hour after stepping out of her bath, Amelia left her bedroom, fully dressed and with her hair in an intricate design she would never had been able to do herself. It turned out Mrs. Bannon had been a lady's maid many years before and knew enough to capture some of the newer styles based on her training. She'd used hot irons to persuade her hair to curl, then drew the bulky mass into a lovely, elaborate bun at the back of her head, with flowers intertwined. She felt like a fairy princess.

After fastening the emerald-green satin mask that matched her gown Amelia took one last look in the mirror and made her way downstairs. Some of the club members had already arrived, several with their wives. The musicians, dressed in proper attire, were setting up in the corner. Her stomach was in flutters thinking about her first ball.

If only Driscoll were here, she mused.

"You are looking splendid tonight, Miss Pence." Dante bowed to her as she took in the transformation from a gaming club to an elegant ballroom. He was dressed in a black domino and a matching mask. Beneath the domino, he wore his usual formal attire.

He was a handsome man, and a favorite of the ladies. From what she'd seen, he spent a great deal of time flirting and teasing the women who visited the club on a regular basis. Amelia was sure he felt comfortable doing so because none of the women who spent time at The Rose Room were of the debutante, looking-for-a-husband ilk. In other words, safe.

From what Driscoll had told her about his brother, as well as what she'd observed herself, Dante had no desire to step into the parson's noose.

She offered the curtsey she'd spent her childhood perfecting and added, "You look quite dashing yourself, Mr. Rose."

He smiled at her for the first time in over a week and extended his arm. "Would you care for some champagne?"

"Yes. I would love some. I've never had it before."

"Ah, then we must correct that oversight." They strolled to the area set up with silver punch bowls filled with both spirited and non-spirited punch, along with a variety of wines, liquors, and champagne. Three extra footmen had been employed for the evening to wander the room with trays of champagne. A fourth temporary employee would be in control of the table holding the liquor.

Dante snatched two glasses and handed one to Amelia. "You certainly look like you belong in such surroundings. Quite comfortable."

She stiffened at his soft words and slight smirk. Whatever did he mean by that? Confused by his statement, she thought it best to merely smile and sip her champagne. "Will the earl join us tonight?"

Dante nodded. "Yes, Lord Huntington was persuaded to leave their new offspring long enough to at least make an appearance." He smirked. "I don't expect to see him for long, however. My sister-in-law is not one who believes anyone but herself can handle the child, and Hunt will want to be right there supporting her.

"Have you seen the baby?" She grimaced as the bubbles from the champagne tickled her nose.

"Ah, yes. Driscoll and I were there when the birthing hysteria began. We felt it best to leave our brother to deal with his wife. However, we did return the next day to bestow our admiration on the urchin."

"A beautiful child, I am sure."

Raised eyebrows and a slight grin was the only answer Dante provided. He looked toward the door. "I believe with Driscoll missing, I needs make myself available to greet the members." He bowed in her direction. "If you will excuse me."

She watched him walk off and looked around to see where the other women from the club were. Margie and Betsy were speaking with two men across the room, and she decided to join them.

Amelia felt herself more observer than attendee. Everyone seemed to know everyone else. Being a non-member of Polite Society due to her isolation most of her life, she knew no one.

But she did enjoy watching the activities and conversing with Betsy and Margie. She hummed and swayed with the music until a man sauntered up to them, offered a slight bow and stared directly at her. "Well, who have we here?"

Betsy giggled and waved at Amelia. "Ah, since this is a masquerade ball, my lord, you must wait until midnight when everyone removes their masks."

Amelia felt a jolt of panic. They were to remove their masks at midnight? Why hadn't anyone told her this? She could not take a chance on someone recognizing her. For heaven's sake Mr. Lyons might even be here! It would behoove her to keep track of the time and make sure she was upstairs, safe and sound in her bedchamber when the clock struck twelve. She giggled. Like Cinderella.

The young lord who Betsy chastised for asking for names looked at Amelia. "May I request a dance, my dear?"

She grew cold at his request. Addressing her so familiarly unnerved her. She was beginning to believe since Driscoll was unable to attend, she might have been better off passing on the ball. However, since denying the man a dance would appear quite odd, she attempted a smile. "Of course. I would enjoy a dance."

"Ah, a waltz, my favorite." He extended his elbow, and she rested her hand on his arm. They moved to the area that had been set aside for dancing. The dance began and the first thing she noticed was he was too close, held her too tight. She attempted to push herself back, but his arm clamped around her waist and he merely laughed. She could smell the alcohol coming from his breath.

He leaned in close to her ear. "I might not know your name, little lady, but I know you're the dealer here who has all the men wagering on who you are. How about we take a walk outside? You could give me a peek at your lovely face under the mask. Help me win the bet."

She moved her head to one side, her eyes watering at the stench of liquor coming from his mouth. The panic started in her chest at his words. There were wagers on who she was? She must give serious consideration to leaving her employment sooner than she had hoped. "No, sir. I am fine here."

Once again, she attempted to put space between them. "What's the matter, sweetheart, I thought all you girls liked being held close."

Anger swelled in her stomach. "I am not one of the girls who like to be held tight, sir. In fact, I believe I prefer to end this dance now." She tugged and apparently taking him off guard, he released her.

"Now wait a minute. I have money. I can pay you."

Her hand itched to slap his insolent face, but rather than make a scene, she walked as quickly as she could from the man, dodging other dancers as she fled.

"Miss Pence?" Dante's voice managed to break through the pounding of her heart. He took her hand to halt her escape. "Is everything all right?"

Taking a deep breath, she turned and offered him a bright smile. "Everything is fine. I think I just need a breath of fresh air."

"I will be happy to escort you." He studied her carefully.

She shook her head. "No. There is no need for you to do that. I will just step outside for a minute or two."

"If you are sure. . ."

"I am," she snapped, anxious to escape.

She hurried away, just wanting to leave the room. The crowd had grown somewhat since she'd first come downstairs. She passed two men sitting side-by-side on a comfortable settee with a woman perched on one of their laps. The woman wore face paint, and the neckline of her deep red gown was scandalously low. She leaned over and whispered something in one man's ear, making them both roar with laughter.

This had not been a good idea. She shouldn't have come to this event. She didn't know why, but she felt frightened, and not just because of the scoundrel who she'd danced with. For the first time since she'd arrived at The Rose Room all those weeks ago, she felt unsafe.

She made it as far as the front door and took a deep breath of the misty air. She moved down the few steps and rubbed her palms up and down her arms, sorry she hadn't thought to go upstairs first and grab her cape.

"Here, miss, you look quite cold." Two men in masks, obviously headed for the ball approached the doorway. One of them removed his cape and went to swing it around her. "This will keep you warm."

She froze, her instincts kicking in. Perhaps she hadn't recovered yet from the difficulty inside, but she felt as if something wasn't right. She backed up and turned. "Thank you anyway, but I will just return to the ball."

"No, you won't, you bitch."

She opened her mouth to scream, but before she could, one of the men threw the cape he'd taken off over her head. Before she could even utter a sound, she was picked up and quickly bundled off. Taken by surprise, and with the cape over her head she had no idea which direction they headed.

After about three minutes of her wrestling with the arms that held her tight, her shouts muffled by the cape, she was tossed into a carriage. The door slammed.

She landed on her hands and knees and the vehicle lurched forward.

The cape was ripped off her head as she sat on the floor of the carriage, her knees aching from landing on the hard surface. She pushed the hair out of her eyes, her mask dangling from its ribbons, resting on her heaving chest.

She sucked in a deep breath as she stared into the eyes of her stepbrother, sitting next to Mr. Daniel Lyons, both men grinning with satisfaction.

"Welcome back, sister."

## 17

*D*ante sat behind Driscoll's desk in the office, tamping down his need to yawn, while Lady McDaniel continued her tirade about a missing necklace.

"My lady, I'm afraid there is nothing I can do about your missing necklace right now. There are over a hundred people downstairs and conducting a proper search would be impossible. Can you tell me the last time you saw your necklace?"

Frankly, he found it hard to believe that the necklace she described could fall off her neck without her immediately noticing it.

"I didn't notice it missing until I returned from the ladies' retiring room."

Dante glanced at the clock on Driscoll's desk. "And am I to assume you checked there before summoning me?"

She lifted her chin as if he were a ninnyhammer. "Of course."

"Good. Then we will begin to usher guests out shortly. I suggest you return to your home and we will do a thorough search first thing in the morning when the light is better and the room empty. I will send word to you as soon as we find it."

Lady McDaniel stood, taking her husband's hand as she rose. She used the opportunity to look down at him, which was a favorite pastime of ladies of the *ton*, since they never wanted him to forget he was a bastard and not accepted in polite society. Unless they were attempting to lure him to their bed, then the interaction was quite different.

"Very well. However, I must tell you if the piece is not returned by ten in the morning next, I will summon Scotland Yard."

Dante nodded and clutching the rough sketch he'd made from Lady McDaniel's description of the necklace, followed them out the door, reminding himself once again of the reasons they did not permit ladies in the club.

The footmen and security guards had done a good job of clearing out the room while he'd conversed with Lady McDaniel. He personally ushered the couple out the door with further assurance that the necklace would be found.

He walked slowly through the room and eyed the table with the bottles of liquor and decided a drink was just the thing to bring the night to an end. For some reason this ball had not gone as well as other years. Possibly because Hunt was only able to stay a short time and Driscoll was tied up with Home Office business, leaving him with the burden by himself.

He filled a glass and leaned against the wall. "Summon all the employees," he said to Marcus as he returned from escorting the last of the guests out the door. Lord Bentworth had a bit of a problem leaving and Marcus had to encourage him to let the night go.

Once they had all gathered, Dante stood on the third step of the staircase and addressed them. "We had an expensive necklace go missing tonight. Tomorrow I want everyone down here by nine o'clock—yes in the morning," he grinned at the moans. "We will need to do a complete search of the building."

He waved at the group, his eyes glancing around the room. "Off to bed with you. Once the necklace has been found we will clean up this mess. No need to do it tonight."

The employees quickly disbursed, leaving him still sipping his brandy and cursing all necklaces and the self-important ladies who wore them. Especially those worn by women who visited his club and lost them.

While he was cursing women, he might as well include Miss Amelia Pence since she occupied the bedroom where he could stay for the night instead of trudging home only to return early in the morning.

He then realized she was not at the meeting he just held. She did look a bit uncomfortable the last time he saw her, so most likely she retired early. With a loud, ungentlemanly yawn, he left the building and returned home.

\* \* \*

DRISCOLL THREW DOWN THE PENCIL, removed his spectacles and rubbed his very tired eyes. The decoding was not going well. He and the other two men who had been brought in to work on it were as baffled as they had been at the beginning.

Mr. Michael Taylor and Sir Stuart Wilson had been as enthusiastic about delving into the project as he when they'd begun. It was always enjoyable to use one's brain to thwart another man's idea of coding.

A full week and a half later they were still stymied. As bad as that frustration was to abide, the endless notes from Sir Phillip inquiring as to their progress only added to the tension in the room.

The most successful part of the project was

acknowledging to himself that not only did he miss Amelia as much as he thought he would, but he was more determined than ever to have a serious conversation with her about their future. And yes. He'd decided they had a future. Together. Soon.

But presently there seemed a good possibility that the future he intended would happen when they were too old to stand before the vicar. Or climb into bed.

"I think I have something," Sir Stuart almost shouted.

Driscoll and Michael jumped up and leaned over Sir Stuart's shoulder. "What have you found?" Driscoll asked.

"This." Sir Stuart pointed to a paper with numbers he'd arranged, that while not making sense, were at least readable.

Driscoll picked up the paper and studied it. "This isn't it. But we're close." He walked back to his chair and pulled out a fresh piece of paper. With determination to get the assignment finished, he wrote and arranged and re-arranged for about an hour.

Finally. Taking a deep breath, he leaned back and looked over at his co-workers. "It's done."

They scrambled over in his direction and stared at the sheet. After a few minutes Michael slapped him on his back. "Well done, old boy. I believe you have done it. Now all we have to do is decode that stack of papers and we're finished."

Because of the sensitivity of the project, once they cracked the code, they were to interpret the messages contained in the papers that had been confiscated from revolutionaries.

Driscoll looked over at the stack and groaned. Even with three of them working, it would most likely take at least four days to decode it all. He shook his head. "Let's get started, then."

* * *

AMELIA KICKED, scratched and bit her way out of the carriage. Screaming meant nothing since they took her to a small cottage deep in the woods somewhere outside of London.

At least they hadn't tied her up and blindfolded her. They also hadn't responded to her struggling by harming her. But then, she was sure Lyons didn't want a mistress suffering from bruises.

"Settle down, girl," Randolph said.

She lowered her head, attempting to bite his hand. He tightened his hold around her middle that almost took her breath away.

Lyons opened the door to the cottage and Randolph carried her in. He released her and she ran across the room, leaning against the wall. "Don't either of you come near me."

"I'm going to have quite a bit of fun taming your sister, Newton." Lyons grinned at Randolph.

"If you come near me, I will cut off your bollocks." She had no idea where her knowledge of that word came from, or what she would use to accomplish the deed, but was satisfied to see Lyons pale at her remark.

He rubbed his hands together. "We will see about that. All in due time, my dear." Lyons slapped Randolph on the back. "You may leave now. I have this all in hand."

Amelia raced across the room and jumped on Lyons back, pounding him with her fists. She attempted to bite his ear, but he grabbed her wrist and swung her around as if she weighed no more than a child's rag doll.

"You will behave yourself or regret it." He shoved her away and she landed on her hands and knees again. He raised his fist. "Keep that in mind."

Randolph cleared his throat. "Lyons, I would have a

word with you outside." He gestured with his head toward the door.

Lyons turned to Amelia. "Don't try anything stupid."

The two men left the cottage and Amelia dropped into a soft comfortable chair. Her thoughts raced through her mind, mostly focused on how she would get away from Lyons.

She looked around the large room which appeared to be a combination sitting room and dining room. There were a few windows, but even if she were able to climb out of one of them without getting caught, she had no idea where she was or how to get help.

Her head whipped around at the sound of shouting coming from outside the cottage. She stood and walked quickly to the door, leaning her ear against the worn wood.

"A deal is a deal, Newton. If you renege your reputation will be ruined. I will make certain of that." Lyons voice came through quite clearly.

Was Randolph finally admitting his mistake in offering her as a wager and trying to talk Lyons out of taking her as his mistress? For a moment she smiled, thinking perhaps he was not such a bad sort after all. His next words quickly dispelled any respectable qualities she had begun to bestow upon her wretched stepbrother.

"All right. If you agree to release me from the debt so I can hold an auction, I will pay you your wager plus ten percent."

"No. I want half your profits."

Amelia's jaw dropped. *Auction*! Randolph was going to auction her off like a prize bull, or a thoroughbred at Tattersalls?

"Half?" Randolph sounded outraged.

"Half."

"It will take more time to set it up, then. We will

need at least fifty or more men." Randolph's voice took on a whiny pitch.

"Don't panic, Newton. We don't need anywhere near that number. And as long as we keep the chit here, we have all the time we need," Lyons returned.

She moved away, having heard enough. They were going to keep her here as a prisoner while they set up an auction? She didn't know whether to laugh or scream at the absurdity of it.

She walked around the cottage, looking for anything she could use as a weapon. There was a heavy vase, but she feared if she tried to hurl it at one of them, she'd only drop it on her foot.

A search in the kitchen turned up a spoon as well as a heavy pan. Like the vase, she would most likely harm herself if she tried to use the pan as a weapon. However, she slipped the spoon into the top of her stocking.

Did she really think she could spoon someone to death?

She wandered back to the chair and slumped down, the sound of Randolph and Lyons' voices still raised.

Drawing in a deep breath, she sat straight up, her heart pounding.

*Driscoll.*

If only she could somehow get word to him.

Then she laughed, the hysteria building. Yes, of course. Even if she could get word to The Rose Room, he was working on a special assignment for the Home Office at a place unknown even to his brother.

In her desire to keep everything a secret, Driscoll had no idea who she was, where she came from, and who her wretched stepbrother was. He would no doubt believe she had simply disappeared much like she had appeared through a window on a rainy night.

Why was it just now that she realized she could trust him? Why was it just now that she realized she most likely had fallen in love with him, but would probably never see him again?

Swiping angrily at her tears, she raised her head when the door opened.

Randolph stood in front of her, his hands on his hips. "We have a change of plans."

"Oh, thank you. You will be returning me to The Rose Room, then?"

"No. But we can't keep you here for as long as we need to, so we will be traveling back to London once we've had some sleep."

Amelia jumped up and strode to the door to the small bedroom she'd seen when she returned from listening to them argue. "I will sleep here." She closed the door, then dragged a small wooden chair over and tucked it under the doorknob.

She didn't remove any of her clothing, including her dance slippers, and placed the spoon under the pillow, giggling hysterically at her only implement of defense. Despite her fears and anger, she was adrift in sleep within minutes.

* * *

"WHAT THE BLOODY hell do you mean she's disappeared?" Driscoll dropped his satchel at his feet and glared at his brother.

"I don't mean to be flippant, brother, but that is precisely as I said. She's disappeared. Gone. No longer here."

Driscoll turned in a circle and ran his fingers through his hair. "When?"

"The night of the ball."

His head jerked up. "Wasn't that last week?"

"Yes."

Driscoll lowered his voice, his hands plastered on the desk in front of Dante. "Are you telling me Amelia disappeared a week ago and you didn't see fit to send a message to me through Sir Phillip?"

"Why?"

"I'm going to take a deep breath to keep me from going for your throat. Not only is she an employee, but you know my feelings for her are more than that."

"No. Actually, I did not know. I suspected, but. . ."

"Stop!" The blood pounding in his head was bringing on a tremendous headache. Amelia was gone. Disappeared. No one would convince him she left on her own volition.

"Have you notified Scotland Yard?"

Dante leaned back in his chair and crossed his arms over his chest. "There is something else you should know before you insist on calling in the authorities." He hesitated for a minute, then continued. "A very expensive necklace went missing the same night your Miss Pence did."

Driscoll's stomach dropped. "What does that mean?"

"I don't know. But since we knew nothing about the girl, why for all intents and purposes she appeared to be in hiding while refusing to tell us anything about herself, I find it suspicious that both she and the necklace disappeared the same night."

"Have you searched her room?"

"Briefly. I didn't want to invade her privacy. I will tell you the necklace has not been found since the ball, and someone needs to search her room. Since you seem, shall we say, attached to the girl, I will leave that up to you."

Driscoll strode from the office where he'd been speaking with Dante and entered Amelia's room. Like a man possessed, he went through all her belongings, noting she left everything behind.

Dante leaned against the wall while Driscoll pulled out clothing, shoes, undergarments, hair clips, tossing them on the floor, his search becoming more frantic by the minute. He waved at the growing pile on the floor. "Do you honestly believe Amelia left here under her own power and took none of her things with her?"

Dante shrugged. "She's done it before."

Driscoll growled at him and knelt to look under the bed. He swept his arm in a wide arc and touched a box. He pulled it out and flipped the top off.

Sucking in a deep breath, he shook the box and thrust it at his brother. "Do you still think she absconded with the necklace? There are numerous shillings and a few farthings in here—saved from her earnings I would say. I hardly think a thieving young woman would steal an expensive necklace that she would be forced to sell, and then disappear leaving behind all her belongings, and this money."

Driscoll stood and tossed the box on the bed. "Something's happened. Whatever or whomever she was running from has caught up to her."

*F*or as quickly and unexpectedly as Amelia had been bundled off from London to a place unknown, she was then whisked back to London the next morning.

She slept almost the entire trip since the two men had forced her to drink laudanum. Her gown was stained with it, since she spit it out, then refused to open her mouth until Lyons held her nose so she had no choice but to open her mouth to get some air.

At least they had left her alone during the night. Not once had she heard any noises coming from the other room, and the chair she'd placed in front of the door-knob never moved.

Amelia tried her best to stay awake, to think of a way to escape the two devils, but the drug had done its job. She was helped out of the carriage and then her arms were slung over the two men's shoulders as they practically dragged her up the steps to Randolph's house.

She cringed, knowing if anyone saw them they would assume she was drunk and ready to allow these two men to have their way with her. She was grateful that so few people in the neighborhood, even in all of

London for that matter, knew her. On the other hand, Randolph's reputation couldn't get worse, so he wouldn't care.

After dropping her ignominiously on the bed in her former room, the men left her after locking the door. She continued to sleep.

It was around dusk when she awoke. Her mouth felt like she'd drank from the Thames, and her body ached. No doubt they didn't do much to secure her while she slept in the carriage, and the bumps along the way caused bruises in various parts of her body.

She climbed out of the bed and made her way over to the dresser where a fresh pitcher of water sat. It unnerved her to think one of the men might have brought the water while she slept. Hopefully, they'd gotten one of the housemaids to do that duty.

After washing her face and brushing her hair with one of the brushes she had left behind when she'd fled, she felt a bit better. And very hungry.

She pounded on the door until finally it opened. Randolph stood there, an annoyed look on his nasty face.

"I would like something to eat. Or is it your intention to stave me to death?"

He pushed his way in, and she walked to the other side of the bed, keeping her distance.

"No. Now that you're awake, we'll have something sent up to you."

Amelia raised her chin. "Frankly, I prefer to leave and find my own meal."

There was no doubt he was well on his way to being in his cups. He swayed slightly and waved his hand in the air, then quickly grabbed the bedpost to hang on. Yes, he was definitely feeling the effects of too much spirits.

He pointed his finger at her. "Let me make this clear, dear sister—"

"—I am not your sister."

He bowed and again almost lost his balance. "Step-sister, then." He burped. "You will remain here until the auction."

Since they'd never discussed it in front of her, she feigned ignorance. "Auction?"

Randolph snapped his fingers, again, grabbing the bedpost for purchase. She had the feeling she could walk over and with one shove to his shoulder he would be on the floor.

Where was Lyons? If he wasn't in the house, she could very well escape. Almost as if he'd read her mind, Randolph said, "Don't think you will get out of here until we're ready to release you. I have both footmen alerted that you are unbalanced, and they are not to let you leave the house." He grinned and her stomach roiled. "For you own safety, of course. I wouldn't want anything to happen to my beloved step-sister."

Amelia quickly glanced around the room, looking for some sort of a weapon to use on the two footmen if she managed to get past Randolph. Just as her eyes landed on the iron poker next to the fireplace, Lyons sauntered into the room. He appeared to be less inebriated than her stepbrother.

"Ah, our lovely prize has awoken." He turned to Randolph. "Why didn't you summon me? Have you told the lovely Miss Amelia what our plans are?"

"Was just about to, old friend." He burped and closed his eyes briefly.

Lyons cast a reproachful glance in Randolph's direction. "You need to cut down on the brandy if we are going to do this right. We must make plans and you can't do that if you're always reaching for the bottle."

Randolph raised his arm to wave the comment off. He lost his balance, fell to the floor and immediately began to snore.

"Get him out of my room," Amelia said.

Lyons grinned at her. "All in good time, my dear."

"Don't 'my dear' me. I have no intention of going along with your 'plans.'"

Lyons walked closer to her and she backed up, stopping when she reached the wall. "Don't come any closer or you will regret it." She'd learned years ago how and where to strike a man to leave him crying like a babe.

"Hmm. It seems our little prize has a mean streak. That would make you more attractive to a certain sort of gentleman. We must remember that when we advertise our auction."

"It won't work."

Lyons raised his eyebrows. "Indeed? And why is that?"

"Because I won't go along with it. As I said, I know how to defend myself."

He moved a step closer, and she tensed, getting ready to knee him in the groin.

"Ah. I can see you are preparing to harm me." He tsked and shook his head. "We can't have that now, can we?"

Abruptly he turned on his heel and walked to the door. "I will send dinner up to you and have one of the footmen remove Newton here." With those curt words, he walked past the threshold and slammed the door.

Amelia slid down the wall and collapsed into a heap on the floor. She wrapped her arms around her legs, hugging her knees to her chest. For the first time since they grabbed her outside of The Rose Room, she cried.

\* \* \*

Driscoll fisted his hair in frustration for what seemed like the hundredth time as he paced his office. He grew more frantic by the minute. According to his calculations, Amelia had been missing six days.

The first thing he did after Dante gave him the news

was clip his brother on the chin. Hard enough to make his point, not hard enough to put him out of service. Then he went to Scotland Yard to gain their help.

Even before he arrived, he knew that it was most likely a futile trip. When the officer began to question him, he felt ridiculous. No, he wasn't completely sure Miss Amelia Pence was her real name. No, he didn't have any prior address for her. No, he knew nothing of her family. No, he didn't know if she had friends.

He didn't mention the necklace because he knew in his heart she didn't take it. Dante was still working on that one.

The only time the officer seemed interested was when Driscoll told him she left all her belongings behind, even the money she was saving.

He took down the information, but he smirked when he said most likely the young lady disappeared because she grew tired of him. Only the thought of spending time in jail kept him from planting a facer on the officer.

Because of his time working for the Home Office, he was deeply behind in his work. Although he tried his best, he couldn't concentrate long enough to get anything done. Finally, Dante hired someone to help with the ledgers.

*Amelia. Where are you?*

He spent every night wandering the club, looking at faces. Trying to see if anyone looked smug. Or uncomfortable. Listening for words in conversations he could question. Most of the time the club was open, he stood against the wall, a brandy in his hand that he rarely sipped, watching Amelia's table. Marcus had agreed to take it over until they could find someone else.

It was on the eighth day after her disappearance that he got his first clue. He watched Dante make his way across the room, heading directly toward him. He gestured with his head and Driscoll followed him to a small room where they stored gaming supplies. "What is it?"

"I just heard some rumors about an auction being held in two days."

Driscoll shook his head in confusion. "An auction? Horses?"

"No. A woman."

Driscoll felt all the blood leave his head to the extent he felt lightheaded. "What have you learned?" His lips were so stiff with fear the words barely made it past his lips.

"Apparently Lord Newton has a step-sister who he is auctioning off."

The blood returned to his head, and on the way setting his heart to pounding. "Auction her for what?" His voice was so low it was a wonder Dante even heard him. It was either that or shout so loud they would hear it in Bath.

"I think you probably know." He grabbed Driscoll's arm as he meant to move past him. "Stop Brother."

"It has to be her."

"We don't know that for sure. Since the event takes place in two days, I suggest we do some investigating and find out if it's Amelia. Even if it isn't her, we need to alert the authorities."

"No. I don't want the authorities involved. I don't want this story to spread more than it has. I suggest the first thing we do is find out who Newton's stepsister is. I don't travel in Society much, but I never heard of a sibling belonging to Newton."

"Apparently Lyons is involved in this, too."

"Daniel Lyons? That cur?" Driscoll smacked his palm with his fist. "When this is over, I shall beat both of them to a pulp."

Dante shook his head. "No. You won't, because if this is Amelia, we need to keep it as quiet as possible. She is a viscount's stepsister, and who knows what status to which she was born. She should have her place in Society and possibly even a Season to secure a husband. If any of this gets out, she is ruined."

"Surely you are not serious?" Driscoll said, aghast. "Have you not been listening to me? I have every intention of offering for her as soon as she is found. I will protect her with my name. No one would dare cast aspersions on her. She will have the Earl of Huntington as a brother-in-law."

Dante grinned. "And me, as well. Except I'm the bastard."

"Stop. I always hate when you do that. You were raised right along with me and Hunt. Father treated you no differently."

"Ah, but mama."

"Was understandably upset by your arrival. But I think she did her best to overcome that."

Dante remained silent. Despite being distracted by Amelia, he still noticed the shift in Dante's manner.

Not wishing to delve into that right at the time, he said, "In any event, we have two days to find out more about this affair. If it is Amelia, we need to learn where it is to be held, and who can secure an invitation."

"If it is her, we will not be offered invitations, I am sure." Dante rested his hand on Driscoll's arm. "She is an employee of The Rose Room. If she was indeed taken from here, we are the last people Newton and Lyons would want involved."

Driscoll nodded. "I will go to a few clubs right now. See if I can pick up some natter. Since this is illegal, I am sure it is being kept confidential."

Dante nodded. "I know you will be of no use to me or the club until you get this matter settled, so go on. I will be here for the rest of the night. If you need more time, I will prevail upon Hunt to step in for a couple shifts."

Driscoll slapped Dante on the back and left the club.

His first stop was White's, by far the most popular club of the peerage. He took a seat in a small group of gentlemen, most of them known to him.

"Rose!" Lord Sterling offered a greeting. "Not used to seeing you here. Don't you have a club to run?"

"I do. Everyone is entitled to time off." He waved at a footman to bring him a brandy.

Sir Grant Johnson leaned forward. "I hear you have a woman working one of your tables."

Driscoll's stomach muscles tightened. "Yes. We did. She is no longer working for us."

Sterling raised his brows. "Indeed? I was just there a couple weeks ago, and she was working."

Driscoll shrugged, not wanting to put too much emphasis on Amelia. "Employees come and go. We're used to it." Which was, of course, a lie since they rarely lost an employee.

"I heard she was a fine piece of baggage." Sir Grant wiggled his eyebrows and Driscoll had to squelch the desire to pummel his face. If he were to get any worthwhile information, he had to get off the subject of Amelia. All he'd accomplished was to increase his agitation.

They bantered for a while and despite his best attempts, when nothing was forthcoming that Driscoll could use, he excused himself and made his way to Brooks's.

Once he joined a small group of men, he decided to be more aggressive about seeking information. He swirled the brandy in his glass. "I heard some rumors about an auction."

Mr. Joshua Tilton leaned in and whispered. "Not supposed to talk about it. Illegal, you know." He looked around as if expecting the authorities to swarm the building and haul him off. "I understand the invitations are hard to come by, but, if you want more information, talk to Lyons. Or maybe Newton. They're running it."

*Bloody hell.* He obviously could not talk to the two of them since he suspected they were the ones holding Amelia.

"Anyone know the chit?" Driscoll felt dirty even asking the question. The thought of a young girl, any young girl, not just Amelia, being auctioned off to the highest bidder was repugnant.

Mr. David Archer also leaned forward. "From what I've heard it's Newton's step-sister."

Driscoll let out a low whistle. "I didn't know Newton had a step-sister."

"I saw her once," Archer said, downing his glass of brandy. "Newton threw one of his parties. She was living there at the time. She made a quick appearance, but nippily left when she saw what kind of parties Newton runs." He winked. "If you know what I mean." He paused. "Pretty piece."

Driscoll's mouth dried up. He was close. Very, very close. As nonchalantly as possible, he said. "Oh? What does she look like?"

Then he sat there with his heart thundering in his chest and his head pounding while Archer described Amelia.

## 19

"What's the latest count?" Lyons leaned over Randolph's shoulder and peered at the list of auction attendees, which was only two days off.

"Eighteen, if we include Lord Ashley-Cooper. He hasn't confirmed yet, but he has shown a great deal of interest," Randolph said.

"He will be here, of that you can be sure. He's an old lecher and would love to get his hands on some young flesh."

Again, Randolph's stomach roiled. The closer they got to the auction, the more he regretted getting involved with it. Truth be known, he also felt nothing but remorse for starting the whole thing by offering Amelia as a wager to Lyons. What had seemed like a good idea at the time in his drunken state had now awakened a long-silenced conscience that he thought was dead and buried.

What would his father think? He was quite fond of Amelia, thought of her as his own daughter.

Almost as if he'd spoken the words out loud, Lyons looked at him with a tightened jaw. "You are not thinking about reneging once again on our deal, are you, Newton?"

Randolph shook his head. "No. Not at all. I was just thinking of any others to whom we can extend an invitation." He sighed. It didn't matter how much it troubled him to auction off his stepsister, he didn't have the blunt to pay Lyons and his credit with the usual moneylenders was nil.

"I just want to make sure Amelia goes to someone who won't abuse her."

Lyons straightened and glared at him. "You are having second thoughts, aren't you?"

"Well, she is my sister. I mean stepsister. And my ward. It does make one feel a tad uncomfortable."

Lyons slapped him on the back. "You will get over it when you see how much the chit brings in. If things go as I believe they will, you'll have enough to continue your lifestyle until you can find a wealthy wife. We have some pretty deep pockets on our list."

Randolph nodded, knowing Lyons spoke the truth. He didn't have a feather to fly with and if he wanted to find a rich wife, he needed the blunt to update his wardrobe, purchase flowers, theater and museum tickets. All the things young ladies expected when they were being courted.

If he could only push from his mind the image of a young Amelia when she first arrived at Newton Manor with her mother after the former Viscount Newton had married the woman. Amelia had been a pretty little girl, shy and quiet. As she'd stepped out of the carriage and looked up at him, she gave him a soft smile. She'd been dressed in a blue flowered dress, white stockings and black shoes. A blue ribbon had tied her golden blonde hair back.

His father had developed quite an affection for the girl, which Randolph was young enough and foolish enough to resent.

Assuming Randolph held the same fondness for Amelia, the former viscount had handed her guardianship and the responsibility for her welfare to him. He'd expected Randolph to give her a Season and find her a suitable husband with the dowry he left. Instead, his son had spent the dowry and was now auctioning her off as a mistress to cover the cost of his debauched lifestyle.

Another stab at his conscience, knowing the old viscount had depended on him to do the right thing.

He sighed. "Very well. I have no intention of going back on my word." He looked up at Lyons with a self-derisive sneer. "You know I am an honorable man."

* * *

DANTE AND DRISCOLL arrived at the drawing room in Hunt's London townhouse to the sound of wails from a baby and sobs from its mother. They took one look at each other and turned on their heels to leave.

"Don't. Go. Anywhere." Hunt stood with his hand on Diana's shoulder as she attempted to calm the screaming child in her arms.

"Isn't there a nurse?" Dante asked, staring with wide eyes at the amount of noise coming from such a small body.

"She went to fetch s-something to ease Alicia's stomach. She a-appears to have a problem with d-digestion." Driscoll could hardly hear Diana's broken reply over the screams.

"Ah, here we are, little darling." A rounded woman, somewhere in her fifties, who must have been the nurse, entered the room with a bottle of brown liquid. "A tad bit of chamomile and ginger will set her little body to straights."

She lifted the sobbing child from Diana's arms, who then wiped the tears that had been streaming down her own cheeks. She stood, wobbling a bit until Hunt gripped her elbow. "I think you should rest for a while, my love. You look a tad worn out."

Diana merely nodded at her two brothers-in-law and walked with Hunt out of the drawing room. "I shall be right back," Hunt threw over his shoulder.

"Blasted things, babies," Dante said as the room quieted down.

"But a blessing as well," Driscoll added.

Dante smirked. "You never would had said that two months ago. I think you have fallen hard, dear brother."

Perhaps he had. The idea of Amelia as his wife and swollen with his child caused as much joy as the idea of him not rescuing her in time caused him excruciating pain. No matter. Even if they were too late to rescue her from the fate Newton planned, Driscoll would still take her as his wife. After he killed, slowly and painfully, whoever 'won' her in the auction.

The two brothers sat in silence, sipping on the tea a footman brought to the room shortly after Hunt left.

"Diana is settled, and the babe is already asleep." Hunt rubbed his hands together as he entered the room. He walked to the tea cart and fixed a cup of tea and then sat across from his two brothers. "What news do you have?"

They had visited with Hunt when Driscoll had first learned of Amelia's disappearance. As a peer, and member of the House of Lords, Hunt had many contacts that he used to uncover anything he could about the missing woman. Before his questions had brought any information, Driscoll had learned about the auction and the woman being offered, who he knew to be Amelia.

"The auction is to be held in two days. As far as I have been able to ascertain, the event is by invitation only, and given our contentious relationship with Newton and the fact that he had Amelia kidnapped from our club, I don't think any of our names are on the coveted list."

Unable to sit still, which is how Driscoll's days—and nights—had been since he'd returned from the Home Office assignment, he jumped up and began to pace. "I don't wish to involve the authorities since Amelia's name will be dragged through the mud and any chance she would have of a normal life thereafter will be nil."

Hunt eyed his brother with smugness. "And am I to assume you wish the thereafter life to be with you?"

Driscoll stopped and nodded. "Yes. I intend to offer for her the minute she is free of Newton's clutches." He glared at Dante. "No matter what the outcome is." He turned back to Hunt. "And Newton won't dare object to the match, given he is her guardian, as long as I assure him no legal ramifications would befall him."

"What is our plan, then?" Hunt asked before popping a small sandwich into his mouth.

"Driscoll's suggestion of beating the man to a pulp before he can hold the auction was not the best, I think." Dante grinned at his brother.

"Why not?" Driscoll asked. "We know he has her, we know for what purpose. Why not just walk up to his house, barge our way in and rescue her?"

"Little brother, you are not thinking clearly. One cannot barge into a peer's home, snatch one of the residents and expect there will be no repercussions," Hunt said.

"Anyway," Dante added, glancing sideways at his brother, "I think our best move is to wait until the night of the auction." He leaned forward, resting his elbows on his knees. "We have to get her before the bidding starts. Once a gentleman has been awarded—I hate that term—the girl, it will be harder to get her out. I would prefer to have as little commotion as possible."

"What if I visited with Newton and offered to pay

whatever he thought he would gain from the auction?" Driscoll asked.

"Then you would buy her, like one of the attendees?" Dante snapped, his brows raised at his brother.

"Of course not," Driscoll snapped back. "The men attending this disgraceful event plan to make her a mistress. I would offer her marriage. If the blunt is enough, he might let her go."

Hunt shook his head and took his last sip of tea. "It won't work. He has a grudge against us for banning him from the club. If he refuses your offer, he will be privy to your desire to have the girl. Our surprise plot to snatch her during the auction will be lost. He will hire guards if you make your intentions known."

Driscoll stopped his pacing. "All right, so what do we do?"

Hunt leaned back in his chair. "Newton will have her locked up, probably with guards, so there is no way to get to her before his event. However, I can't imagine this being a quiet, refined affair. I'm sure there will be plenty of liquor and noise. Once the party gets started, one of us goes in."

"Me," Driscoll said.

Hunt gave a curt nod. "You will have to look around. Don't go in right away. I'm assuming Newton will want to have everyone feeling generous and well into their cups before he starts his auction. Knowing the sort of man who will attend one of these things, they will also be heavy drinkers and free with their blunt."

"Most likely she is locked in her bedchamber. I have no idea where that is, but I'll find it."

Hunt stood. "I have a set of implements you can use that will open any lock in the house."

The earl grinned at his brothers' shocked expressions. "Certainly, you don't think when I visit *ton* parties to gather information for the Crown that they thoughtfully leave all the rooms unlocked?"

"Then I think we're all set," Dante said. "Hunt and I will wait outside with a carriage. Once you have her, find a back or side door to bring her out. If not, you might have to drop her out a window."

"How will you know?" Driscoll asked.

"I will wait at the back of the house where the bedchamber windows are. If you need to drop her, I can do my best to catch her before she lands. But that is a last resort. All of those townhouses have back entrances for the servants and delivery men. If she's lived there before, she must know how to find the back stairs.

"Hunt will be in the front, but down a few houses in his carriage." Dante pointed at Driscoll. "Just don't get so carried away with your lady that you forget me and trot on home."

Driscoll looked at his two brothers who he'd depended on all his life. They'd had their scuffles and flat-out fist fights growing up, but he would do anything for either of them, and it appeared they felt the same way about him. "Thank you. You have no idea how much this means to me."

Hunt grinned and glanced at the ceiling where his wife rested. "Yes. I do. Now if you will excuse me, I feel the need to take a nap."

"A nap!" They both shouted.

"When there is a soft, warm, willing woman in your bed, a nap is always the best way to occupy an afternoon." He waved at them as he left the room. "Be gone with you. I have things to do."

* * *

AMELIA CONTINUED to wring her hands as she paced the bedchamber. Never had she regretted anything more than her decision to not tell Driscoll who she was and what Randolph had planned for her. She was stupid, plain stupid, that was the only thing she could attribute it to.

She could already hear the arrival of the men as they made their way through the front door. Loud, laughing, some of them sounded as if they had already downed an entire bottle of brandy.

Actually, it didn't sound very different from when Randolph had his usual parties. Except she was certain this one did not have any of the loose women he generally invited along as 'entertainment' for his guests.

She let out a hysterical giggle. No, *she* would be the only loose woman at the party. She cringed, thinking of what was in store for her. She'd spent so many hours trying to think of a way to get out of this disaster. Oh God, how could she save herself?

The crowd grew rowdier, and she more panicky, as time went on. She could attempt to run once they let her out of the room, but with all those men downstairs she wouldn't get very far. She had already searched her room completely and found nothing she could use as a weapon. Randolph had stripped it bare before he locked her in.

She had climbed out the window when she'd escaped the last time but since then Randolph had one of the footmen nail it shut, so that way was blocked. And she couldn't break the window because they'd taken all the linens from her bed, which she used the last time to make a rope to climb out. She'd been forced to sleep completely clothed, with a cape wrapped around her to keep from freezing during the night.

In her darkest moments she attempted to tell herself maybe the life Randolph planned for her wouldn't be so bad. Perhaps she would be sold to a nice older man, someone kind, who would treat her well and not demand she share his bed too often.

Oh, God who was she kidding? The life of a mistress was not one of respectability. She would never have children, and if she did, they would be bastards, and no one would accept them. They would grow to hate her.

Her head jerked up at the sound at her door. Were they coming for her already? She looked around frantically, thinking there must be somewhere she could hide. She stopped. It didn't sound like the door was unlocking, it sounded like scratching.

She walked to the door and knelt. The scratching continued. She pressed her ear against the door. An animal? Wonderful. Just want she needed to complete her night. Attacked by a crazed rat.

Suddenly, the door was pulled open, and she tumbled forward.

Right into Driscoll's arms.

---

$\mathcal{D}$riscoll held Amelia in his arms and pressed her head against his chest as she sobbed her heart out and mumbled words he could not understand, clinging tightly to him.

"Shh. It's all right, sweetheart. You must quiet yourself. We have to get you out of here without anyone knowing."

She pulled away and nodded, accepting the handkerchief he handed her. Gripping her shoulders, he leaned back and looked at her as she wiped her wet cheeks. Face paint had been applied to her lovely visage, and her glorious hair hung down almost to her waist. His eyes lowered to see her garbed in a night dress and dressing gown. Both skimpy and both causing his stomach to clench with enough rage to find her brother downstairs and beat the living hell out of him.

Instead, he had to get Amelia away. As quickly as possible. He could never take on all the men drinking, laughing and generally raising hell downstairs. From what he'd seen when he entered the house—the door no longer being guarded as it had been earlier—

Randolph would be upstairs any minute to drag Amelia to the auction before everyone got too drunk to bid.

"Do you know how to access the back stairs?" There didn't seem to be any reason to lower his voice since he would never be heard downstairs.

Still gulping for air, she nodded.

"Good." He stood and removed his jacket, covering her with it. He took her hand and helped her up. "Come. We must leave quickly."

Although he and his two brothers all carried pistols, he preferred not to be forced to shoot his way out of the house.

Taking a deep, shuddering breath, Amelia clung to his hand as she led him down the corridor. Once they reached the door to the back staircase, heavy footsteps sounded from the other end of the corridor. Randolph and his cohorts were coming for her. He broke into a sweat thinking how close he'd come to arriving too late.

"Hurry." He moved in front of her and all but dragged her down the stairs. Since the door to her bedchamber was no longer locked, it wouldn't take the men long to discover Amelia gone.

They stepped out into the night air and Dante strode up to them.

"We have to get out of here. They will have just learned that Amelia is gone." With a swoop of his arms, Driscoll picked Amelia up and crushing her to his chest, they ran for the carriage.

A roar broke out behind them from the front door just as they reached the vehicle. Hunt opened the door, and Driscoll all but threw Amelia inside. Once the three men entered the carriage and slammed the door, the vehicle took off, disappearing into the misty night, leaving the angry shouts behind them.

Amelia sat huddled in the corner, tugging the flaps of his jacket together. Although she shivered, he was reluctant to pull her against him to create warmth, not yet sure of her frame of mind. It was a short ride from Newton's house to Hunt's townhouse, so he would wait and give her time.

It had been decided that the most obvious place for Newton to come to demand the return of Amelia would be The Rose Room. Bringing Amelia to Hunt's house also prevented any scandal from erupting since with Lady Huntington present, there would be no question about Amelia's reputation being ruined.

The carriage came to a rolling stop in front of Huntington Townhouse. Hunt stepped out, then Dante. They both headed up the steps. Driscoll turned to Amelia, pushing her abundance of hair behind her ear. "Are you ready to leave?"

She nodded, her eyes as they met his filled with tears. "They were going to auction me off."

"I know, sweetheart. If you wish to discuss it later, we can." He extended his hand. "Come. For now, let's go inside where it is warmer."

He stepped down, turned and took her ice-cold hand in his. Since she was barefooted, he once again carried her up the steps and into the house. Diana stood in the entrance hall, anxiety written on her face. She held her arms out. "Oh, my dear."

Amelia walked straight into Diana's embrace, as if they were long-lost best friends. Apparently even a previously unknown woman was comforting to a woman in Amelia's state.

Diana looked over Amelia's shoulder. "I will bring her upstairs and find something for her to wear. We will meet you in the drawing room."

Driscoll reluctantly nodded and allowed Diana to take Amelia away from him. He watched them ascend the stairs, Amelia's head resting on Diana's shoulder. He understood that she needed the comfort of a woman right now, but he was not going to wait over-long to make his intentions known. No one would ever touch her again.

Once he had Amelia's consent, he would send for a special license, visit with Newton to demand his approval of the match, and visit the nearest vicar. Amelia would never have to worry about taking care of herself for the rest of her life. She would be his and damn anyone who tried to do her harm.

His lips tightened as he turned to join his brothers in the drawing room. He would very much enjoy visiting Newton tomorrow when the cad was feeling the result of his overindulgence, and perhaps the wrath heaped upon him by the thwarted men he'd invited to the auction. He hoped to add significantly to the man's misery.

\* \* \*

AMELIA TURNED and looked at the woman who had brought her upstairs. She remembered seeing her briefly when the earl made a quick visit to the club one evening when Lady Huntington was heavy with child. Amelia had been dealing at the time and didn't get to meet her.

"Amelia—can I call you Amelia?" Lady Huntington said in a soft soothing tone.

"Yes. Of course." Amelia was surprised her own voice worked as well as it did. She'd been crying since she fell into Driscoll's arms and her eyes burned and her nose was stuffy.

"Then you must call me Diana." She smiled warmly and Amelia felt more at ease than she had for days.

"We have a bathing room down the corridor. I had a bath prepared for you, assuming you would like to relax for a bit."

Amelia closed her eyes. "That would be wonderful.

They sprayed me with some sort of perfume that is making me nauseous."

Diana smiled in sympathy. "I noticed."

Thankful that Diana did not wish to question her, Amelia followed her down the corridor to a wonderful room where she could easily spend the next few hours.

A large copper bathing tub sat against one wall, steam from the water misting softly in the air. A small table sat next to the tub with soap and a linen square placed on it. Behind the tub, two towels, large and fluffy, hung on a rack. Amelia groaned at the sight.

"That's what I thought," Diana said with a smile. "I will leave you to your bath." She pointed to a large comfortable chair in the corner opposite the tub. "I placed some clean clothing there for you to change into.

"In a little while I will send my maid up to assist you in dressing. She will bring you down to the drawing room when you are finished."

Tears welled in Amelia's eyes again. "I don't know how to thank you. Or your husband, and Dante. . ." She shook her head, unable to continue.

Diana touched her arm gently. "Be at ease, Amelia. We are all happy to see you safe and away from that horrible place." Taking a deep breath, she opened the door. "Enjoy your bath. I know Driscoll is anxious to see you."

*Driscoll.*

Was he angry with her for not telling him what he'd asked her for weeks? Yes, he rescued her, but that could be because she was an employee and he felt honor-bound to do that.

She removed the horrid night clothes they'd forced her to wear and tossed them in the corner, hoping she would have the enjoyment of burning them. She climbed into the tub, sighing as the warm water enveloped her body. She took the small linen square, rubbed the sweet-smelling soap over it and washed the face paint off. She was appalled at the way they had forced her to dress. A jolt of panic raced through her when she thought about how close she'd come to being presented dressed as a courtesan in front of who knows how many men all eager to bid on her.

She slid down in the water and washed her hair. She scrubbed her skin so hard she thought she would rub it off. No sooner had she'd finished washing than a soft knock on the door drew her attention. "Please come."

A small maid entered and offered her a warm smile. "Good evening, Miss, I am Theresa. Her ladyship asked that I assist you."

She nodded to the young maid. "Thank you. That will be very nice."

Being raised the way she had, she had no problem with the maid helping her out of the tub, drying her off and helping her dress. "I believe they are anxious for you to join them in the drawing room, so may I have permission to fix your hair in such a way that we don't have to wait for it to dry?"

"Yes. That would be fine." She turned so the maid could fasten the back of the gown Diana had left for her. "They are anxious for me?"

Theresa walked around her and smiled. "Actually, Mr. Driscoll is anxious to see you. He has been pacing the drawing room since they arrived."

Theresa had her sit at the small dressing table in the bathing room where she plaited her hair, then wrapped the plaits around her head, fastening them with pins. Looking in the mirror, Amelia could hardly reconcile the woman in the mirror to the one who arrived with face paint, loose hair, and dressed in scandalous night-clothes.

"I have been asked to escort you to the drawing room when we are finished," Theresa said. She looked over Amelia's shoulder and smiled at her in the mirror. "I believe we are ready."

Amelia nodded and stood. They walked the corridor to the stairs that led to the ground floor where the public rooms were located. Amelia's heart began to pound, and she was finding it hard to catch her breath. Driscoll stood on the other side of the imposing, large wooden door.

Would he turn from her in anger? In disgust? Might he tell her she was no longer employed by The Rose Room? Would he insist she return to Randolph with a warning to him to treat her better?

Stiffening her spine, she took a deep breath and stepped through the door the footman opened. Diana, Lord Huntington, Dante and Driscoll ceased their conversation and turned at her entrance. She had to tamp down the urge to flee.

Driscoll walked up to her and took her hands in his. "Are you feeling well, my love?"

She stared into his eyes. Anger?

No. Disgust?

No. Concern?

Yes. Love?

Frighteningly so. She licked her dry lips. "Yes. I am well. Thank you." She turned to Lord Huntington, Diana, and Dante. "I can't express how much I appreciate what you've done for me. I cannot. . ." She stopped, her throat working as she tried to control the tears that threatened to embarrass her.

Diana stood and motioned to her husband and Dante. "I think it is time for us to retire. Dante, if you wish we have a room readied for you."

Dante shook his head. "Thank you, Diana. You are gracious as always. However, I think there is still time for me to stop by The Rose Room." He walked to Amelia. "Welcome back, Miss Pence. 'Twas an interesting night."

She grinned. "Thank you."

The three left the room, closing the door softly behind them. Amelia began to study her feet encased in the soft slippers Diana had provided, not quite sure what to do now that she and Driscoll were alone.

Driscoll placed his finger under her chin and raised her head until she was staring into his eyes. She was still unable to reconcile the emotion she saw there. "Would you care for a drink? Brandy? Sherry? Tea?"

Amelia nodded and ran her palms up and down her arms. "Actually, a brandy sounds very good right now."

He led her to a settee and walked to the other side of the room and poured two brandies. He turned to face her and leaned against the sideboard, his long legs crossed at the ankles as he swirled the brandies and studied her.

She quelled the desire to squirm at his scrutiny. Pushing himself away from the sideboard, he moved forward and took the space alongside her. He handed her the cut crystal snifter, watching her over the rim of his glass as he drank. She took a sip, the liquid burning all the way to her stomach. She sucked in a deep breath and coughed.

Once she had her breath back, he casually stated, "You are no longer an employee of The Rose Room, Miss Pence."

"Miss Smythe," she mumbled. Her shoulders slumped. He *was* angry with her. Probably all the Rose brothers were.

Driscoll raised his brows at the news of her real name. He removed the glass from her hand and placed it, along with his own on the small table in front of them. "Do you know why you are no longer employed?"

She shook her head, unable to speak. Of course, she could think of many reasons, starting with his anger at the secrets she refused to tell him and ending with requiring him and his brothers to rescue her from the clutches of her horrid stepbrother who they had already banned from the club.

Before she could ask for a reason, he slipped from the settee and rested on one knee in front of her. He took her hands in his and looked directly into her eyes. "Miss Amelia Pence—Smythe, if that is your true name —I would be the happiest of men if you would consent to be my wife." He raised her hand to his lips and kissed her fingers, one at a time, while he stared up at her.

*Wife?*

Oh, good heavens, she was about to cry again. She couldn't speak, only nod. Driscoll's grin convinced her he was serious. He pulled her down alongside him on the floor and cupped her face, covering her mouth with his. The passion that exploded in her body would have knocked her to her knees had she been standing.

Driscoll pulled her closer, angling her head so he could take the kiss deeper. His tongue nudged her lips and she gladly opened to him. Their tongues tangled, sweeping, tasting, sucking. Every fear, worry, and rage that had occupied her mind for the past few days vanished like a wisp of smoke on a windy day.

Driscoll pulled back and kissed the sensitive skin on her neck. He moved to her collarbone, nipping, soothing with his lips, his tongue. "I love you, Amelia, and I've wanted you for so long, and dear God, I thought I'd never see you again."

His hands wandered her body, squeezing, caressing, stroking. He cupped her breast and flicked his thumb over her nipple which immediately responded standing straight and hard. Once more he covered her mouth, crushing her to his body. He could not get enough of her. And to think he almost lost her.

Slowly pulling back, he rested his hands on her shoulders. "I want you. Now." He eased forward, his mouth close to her ear and whispered, "Diana mentioned which bedchamber you were given." He kissed her closed eyelids. "Smart woman, my sister-in-law."

Amelia sucked in a breath at what he was suggesting. She looked at him, with all the love that was in her heart. Without hesitation she said, "Yes."

It seemed that was all he needed to hear. Driscoll jumped up, extended his hand to help her rise. He wrapped his arm around her waist and quickly herded her out of the drawing room, up the stairs and down the corridor. Quietly, he opened her bedchamber door. "I will be gone before dawn, so no one needs know," he whispered against her lips.

He pulled her inside and cupped her chin to kiss her once more as the door latch slowly clicked shut.

---

*T*he morning after the auction disaster Newton sat at his breakfast table still dressed in the clothing from the night before. His bleary eyes could barely focus with the throbbing of his head and the roiling of his stomach.

One didn't have to be overly intelligent to guess the Rose brothers had something to do with Amelia's disappearance. Once he was feeling better, he would go to the club and demand they return the chit to his protection. He was her guardian and if he had to invoke the courts, he would do just that.

"My lord, you have a visitor." Stanford, his butler at the door spoke quietly having already received a tongue lashing for speaking too loudly earlier.

Randolph waved his hand. "I'm not receiving." It was most likely another disgruntled guest from the night before wanting to harass him further. It was bad enough that he still owed Lyons the money for the wager and now the man was demanding Amelia as well as fifty pounds for his trouble. Where the devil would he get fifty pounds?

Stanford took his leave and before Randolph could return to his muddled thoughts a scuffle ensued outside the door to the breakfast room. He looked up to see Driscoll Rose looming over him. "Get up, Newton."

"Come to gloat, did you? Well, I intend to visit with my solicitor today and make arrangements to have Miss Smythe returned to my care."

"Your care?" Rose growled. "You call auctioning her off to a bunch of leering, debauched wastrels taking care of her?"

"'Tis none of your business."

Driscoll leaned down, so close Randolph could smell the coffee on his breath. "Stand up."

When Randolph didn't move, Driscoll grabbed him by his cravat and hauled him to his feet. With one swift punch to the gut, Randolph collapsed to the floor, casting up his accounts all over the Aubusson carpet, the last of his finer things—everything else having been sold.

Driscoll grabbed a napkin from the table and dropped it on him, then growled, "Clean yourself up and stand. I'm not finished with you."

If not for the crazed look in his visitor's eyes, Randolph would have curled up into a ball and shouted for Stanford to toss Rose out the door. However, he wiped his mouth and climbed to his feet.

Rose grabbed him again and slammed him into his chair. "Miss Smythe is no longer your concern. She has accepted my hand in marriage."

"Now see here," Randolph sputtered, "she cannot marry without my permission."

"Wrong, Newton. She will and damn your guardianship. And I will explain why." Rose drew out a chair and sat, adjusting his jacket, and resting his ankle on his knee, as if they were having a gentlemanly conversation. "What you attempted to do last night is illegal. Right now, as we have this friendly conversation, my brother is headed to Scotland Yard to file charges against you." He brushed lint off his jacket. "In case you're wondering, we have men willing to step forward and testify as to the events here last night."

"Nothing happened here last night except a gathering of men to enjoy cards and drinking. No different than any other gentlemen's clubs. Or your own gaming club for that matter."

Driscoll shook his head. "Stubborn, aren't you? Well, the men we have already contacted have agreed to testify as to *why* there was a gathering here last night. Miss Smythe is also prepared to swear that you tried first to pay a gambling debt offering her services as a mistress, and then decided to make it a full auction instead." He shook his head. "Not well done, Newton. Illegal. Immoral. Very untrustworthy. Very unguardianly. The courts look down on men who abuse women and take advantage of their wards."

His head pounding even more, and his stomach still prepared to bring up whatever was left, he closed his eyes and shook his head. "What do you want, Rose?"

Driscoll grabbed him by the cravat again and came within inches of his nose. "You will sign the papers I have with me, granting permission for Miss Amelia Smythe to marry Mr. Driscoll Rose, second son of the late Earl of Huntington and brother to the current Earl of Huntington."

Randolph nodded. He knew when he was outflanked and outmaneuvered. How he would pay Lyons remained to be seen but facing the authorities with these ruinous charges left him no choice.

Rose whipped out papers from his pocket and opened them. Laying them flat on the table, he produced an ink pen and handed it to him.

"I am prepared to pay off your debt to Lyons, as well as offer you two hundred pounds once this contract is signed."

Randolph frowned not quite sure he'd heard correctly. "Why would you do that?"

"Because, despite everything, you are Amelia's only family. I want her to be happy and not constantly reminded of the debacle she suffered at your hands every time she sees you at an event." He pulled a small linen sack from his pocket, along with a small piece of paper. "I will give you this money on one condition."

"What is that?" Rose was too cagey to do this just from the goodness of his heart.

He handed him a ticket. "You will accept this for the next boat that sails from Southampton to America. You will use the two hundred pounds in that sack to start a new life for yourself. Hopefully one not as debauched as the one you're leaving behind."

Randolph's heart thumped with both fear and excitement. Leaving his home and country did not appeal but having Lyons off his back and the chance to start a new life gave him something he hadn't had in a long time.

Hope.

"I agree." Randolph quickly signed his name and handed the pen back to Rose. Driscoll tossed the bag at him and handed him the ticket. "I will take care of Lyons." He stood and once more pulled Randolph to his feet. "Just one more thing."

Before Randolph could process what Rose said, the man drew back his arm and smashed his fist into his face, knocking him to the ground again.

He brushed his hands together and stared at him. "Have a nice trip."

*　*　*

DRISCOLL RETURNED to Hunt's townhouse pleased with himself. If Hunt was able to secure the special license, which Driscoll had no reason to believe he wouldn't, the wedding would take place as soon as Amelia and Diana purchased what they felt was suitable wedding attire for his bride. Hopefully that wouldn't take too long.

He intended to take Amelia on a wedding trip but had spent time looking for a decent house to lease, since obviously his flat would not do for a married couple. He'd found two that were acceptable, but he wanted Amelia's opinion before he committed to either of them.

"His lordship is in the breakfast room, Mr. Rose." Peters, Hunt's man at the front door offered a slight bow as he stepped back to allow Driscoll to enter.

Driscoll nodded and took the stairs two at a time to the first floor where the breakfast room was. He entered to see Hunt and Dante seated, sharing a meal. "I guess I am late to the party, then." He moved to the sideboard and filled a plate with eggs, bacon, beans, toast, and smoked trout.

"We have news," Dante said as Driscoll shook out his napkin and placed it on his lap.

"What is that?" He took a sip of tea one of the footmen poured into his cup.

Dante rested his forearms on the table and leaned forward as he studied Driscoll. "Although it was quite hard for me to believe, we have evidence that John, our trusted banker since we opened, was the one shorting Amelia's receipts every night."

Driscoll stopped with his fork halfway to his mouth. "John?" He took a moment to digest that. "I agree, it is very hard to believe that."

Dante's lips tightened. "I'm sorry to say he was also the one who took Lady McDaniel's necklace."

John? Not only was it hard to believe, but the only reason he gave credence to the story was because Dante was the one telling him. He resumed his breakfast as Dante continued.

"Since you were so adamant that Amelia was not stealing from us, I hired an outside man to investigate a couple of weeks before the ball." Dante picked up a paper in front of him and waved it at Driscoll. "This is his report which came yesterday afternoon, but with the activities last night, I never had the chance to discuss it with you.

"Mr. Hartwell, the investigator, had no pre-conceived ideas about the employees since I told him nothing about any of them, so he was able to quickly check the stream of money and with careful observation and counting himself, he discovered where the problem was."

Driscoll shook his head. "Why would John do such a thing? He was well-paid and I always thought of him as a friend."

"A woman, why else? He got himself tied up with a woman who demanded things beyond his reach, so he did what many men do to make fools of themselves," Dante said with a sneer.

Hunt, who had been watching the play between his brothers smiled. "Ah, Dante, I'm not saying either myself or Driscoll are not enamored of our women, but I can understand the playing a fool part."

Dante stared at the two of them and shook his head. "You two are pathetic. I would never have a woman lead me around by a nose ring."

Hunt burst out laughing. "I would not concede that they are leading us around with a nose ring, but one day you will meet your match, brother. Mark my words."

"Never." Dante stood and pushed in his chair. "While the two of you bore each other to death with tales of your love life, I shall visit with my tailor and then spend a few hours at my gentleman's club before opening The Rose Room later." He offered a slight salute and made a quick exit.

"Poor bloke. He has no idea how easy it is to succumb to cupid's bow." Hunt withdrew a folded paper from his jacket pocket. "I have your special license here. I think the ladies are out today gathering what they need to turn your lady into a perfect bride."

"Thank you, brother. I shall contact the vicar today and make the arrangements. Is it acceptable if we hold the ceremony here?"

"Of course. Diana has been happier planning this wedding breakfast than she's been since our daughter was born. It gives her something else to focus on besides how fragile a babe's life is and wondering if every hiccup or cry announces the arrival of a disastrous ailment."

"I'm sure it will pass. As an impartial observer, your daughter looks quite robust to me, and I don't know anything about babies." Driscoll took the paper from Hunt's hand and stood. "Thank you for breakfast. In my optimism for women to quickly put together a stunning outfit for my bride, I shall advise the vicar that the wedding will take place two days hence."

"I will relate that to our ladies when they arrive from their shopping trip."

Driscoll left feeling quite happy. In two days' time he would be a married man, with the woman he would never want to live without by his side. Her despicable stepbrother will shortly depart these shores.

He and Amelia would have a fine wedding trip, followed by settling into their new home. Yes, he had much to look forward to. Who knew a woman, sopping wet and dressed as a man, falling through his window, would end up bringing him such peace and happiness?

* * *

AMELIA HELD her hands up in the air as her wedding dress slithered down her body, the white satin fabric sliding against her skin like a brush of the gossamer wings of a butterfly.

"Oh, this is a beautiful gown, my lady." Amelia's newly hired lady's maid whispered with reverence as she adjusted the shoulders of the dress and moved behind her to fasten it closed.

Amelia had to agree. She glanced at herself in the mirror over her dressing table and smiled. Diana was certainly a force to be reckoned with. They had arrived at Madame Moreau's shop two days before and walked out with a promise for the beautiful gown she now wore. Diana had finagled, charmed and flat-out bribed the modiste to give them a gown she had finished for another woman whose wedding was still a month off.

"Surely you and your seamstresses are talented enough to make another one in plenty of time for—who did you say the gown was for?"

"Miss Frances Richards. A lovely young lady," Madame Moreau said.

Diana, having patronized the woman's shop for years had the upper hand in the negotiations. She also mentioned that the new Lady Amelia Rose would be in dire need of an entirely new wardrobe and, of course, they would consider no one else except the talented Madame Moreau to supply it.

With less reluctance than when they started, Madame Moreau had Amelia try the gown on, and declared with minor adjustments it would be ready in time for her wedding.

"Come and sit here, Miss and I will fix your hair." Emily pulled out the chair in front of the dressing table. Amelia sat and studied her face. In a few hours she would be Lady Amelia Rose. As the daughter of a marquess she would keep her honorific.

Her life would be everything she had thought it would be as a young girl growing up, but very different from what she had expected only a couple of months ago.

*Driscoll.*

She loved her soon to be husband with all her heart. She'd been holding back from him because of her secrets and the fear of what Driscoll would do if she confessed all. She should have known that her soon-to-be husband was not the sort of man who would see her used in such an indecent manner by her stepbrother, regardless of Randolph's status as her guardian. Because of her lack of trust in Driscoll, she almost ended up exactly where she had fled from.

"Oh, my goodness, you look beautiful!" Diana swept into the room, dressed in a lovely rose satin gown. She extended her hand to Amelia and helped her rise. "You have a very nervous groom downstairs, checking his timepiece every two minutes."

"Am I late?" Amelia asked.

"No. He's just anxious to make you his wife." Diana placed her hands on Amelia's shoulders. "I am so happy we will be sisters. I've always wanted one. You are marrying a fine man. I've known Driscoll most of my life. He will make you a wonderful husband."

Amelia smiled. "I am certain he will."

"Ah, you love him," Diana whispered.

"Yes. I do."

Diana eased her arm into Amelia's and moved her forward. "Then let's go save that poor man downstairs from any further angst."

The ceremony itself was almost a blur to Amelia. The line she remembered best was Driscoll's strong words as he held her hands and stared into her eyes.

*With this ring I thee wed; with my body I thee worship; and with all my worldly goods, I thee endow. In the name of the Father, and of the Son, and of the Holy Ghost. Amen.*

Once they were announced as husband and wife, Driscoll leaned close to her ear and whispered, "I love you, Lady Amelia Rose." He then followed with a kiss that had the vicar clearing his throat and the few guests present chuckling.

The wedding breakfast followed, with the three Rose brothers, Diana, and staff members from The Rose Room, drinking champagne and wishing them well. Betsy and Margie were especially giddy at the romance that grew right under their noses.

Amelia looked around at the gathering and then turned to her new husband. She thought of how happy her mother and stepfather would be if they here today to share her joy.

"Is everything all right? You looked sad for a minute." Driscoll clasped her hands and eyed her with concern.

She offered him a bright smile, one filled with the happiness he brought her. "Yes, my love. Everything is fine. Just fine."

# EPILOGUE

"*I* don't understand why you won't let me help you. You're being foolish." Amelia sat on the settee in their drawing room, her back stiff, her arms crossed over her middle, glaring at her husband.

Driscoll ran his fingers through his hair. As much as he loved his wife and was immensely happy with his married state, he feared he would be bald before long, with the way he kept tugging at his hair. No one had ever explained to him how frustrating females could be at times. If not for his occasional visits with Hunt who assured him Amelia, much like his own wife, Diana, was quite normal for a woman, he would view his wife as if she were possessed.

He sat alongside her and took her hands. "Sweetheart, let me repeat myself. Again. You cannot deal cards at the club. You are my wife. It is not proper for you to be out and about in your condition. You are seven months pregnant and can't be on your feet for any length of time."

"I don't care about propriety."

He shook his head no.

"I can sit on a chair."

He shook his head.

"I can take breaks."

He shook his head.

"I will only work half a shift."

He shook his head.

Amelia sighed. "You know, husband of mine, one day your head is going to fly off your shoulders with all the shaking it does."

He smiled.

"You're laughing at me!" Suddenly she broke into tears. Driscoll stood and ran his fingers through his hair. Hunt also told him a pregnant wife was an even more difficult woman to live with.

"Please, honey, don't cry." He sat down again and looked at her very unhappy, red eyes and sighed. He was not going to give in, but perhaps a compromise would work.

"What if I bring you to the club and you work on the books with me?"

She took the handkerchief he handed her and wiped her cheeks. "Really?"

He breathed a sigh of relief when she didn't pick up the book alongside her and hit him on the head with it. "Yes, really."

Her smile broke out like the welcoming sun on a cloudy day. "I would like that. I get so lonely sitting here by myself every night."

He slapped his thighs and stood. "Then it is settled. I will be leaving in a few minutes, so go do whatever it is you need to do before we leave."

With a bit of a struggle, she rose from the chair and waddled off. Despite his reluctance to have her anywhere except at home safe and sound, it would be nice to have her company, and working side by side as they did before.

* * *

IT HAD BEEN months since Amelia had been in the club. When they were first married, she continued dealing until they found a replacement, which took some time since they were also forced to replace John. For a while after that she worked with Driscoll on the books until her pregnancy was confirmed. Then the man she married, who had been so easy to live with and complacent about most things, turned into a stranger who watched her every move, and handled her as if she were made of the finest crystal.

Their very active and satisfying bed sport would have come to an end with his concern about hurting the babe had she not finally purchased some scandalous undergarments and in desperation, seduced him. She still grinned at that evening. One of her best memories.

It felt good to be back where it all started for them. She'd been shocked to receive a letter from Randolph, apologizing for his behavior and asking for her forgiveness. He'd used the money Driscoll had given him to start a small business. She nearly lost her breath laughing when he said he had opened a haberdashery in New York City, and was doing quite well. Life was certainly full of surprises.

She and Driscoll had been working on the ledgers for over an hour when Dante entered the office. "I will be gone for a while."

"Home Office?" Driscoll asked.

"Yes."

"How long?"

"Not sure."

"When?"

"Now."

"We'll handle everything."

With that snappy terse and very confusing conversation, Dante offered them both a salute and left the room.

"Whatever was that about?" She asked.

Driscoll smiled. "Dante has an assignment for the Home Office that may take some time. He will be gone while he's working on it, and I have to cover the club. However, I do have Keniel to help. He's turned into quite a good manager."

"You understood that narrative from the pithy conversation I just witnessed?"

"Yes." He actually looked confused. "Didn't you?"

"Noooo." She dragged the word out. And men thought women were strange creatures.

Driscoll closed the ledger he'd been working on with a definite thud. "Let me speak with Keniel and make sure all is well for tonight." He walked across the office and rested his hip on the edge of her desk, facing her. He leaned over and cupped her chin in his warm hands. "Be ready when I return." He touched her lips lightly, with his, brushing back and forth, just enough to tease, but not satisfy. "I have the need to spend some—shall we say quiet—time with my wife. In our bedroom." With a wink he slid off the desk and she sat there fanning herself as he left the room.

Did you like this story? Please consider leaving a review on either Goodreads or the place where you bought it. Long or short, your review will help other readers discover new authors and make purchasing decisions!

I hope you had fun reading Amelia and Driscoll's love story. *A Lady's Trust* is the second book in the Rose Room Rogues series.

If you missed the first book in the series, Hunt's story, get a copy of *A Scandalous Portrait and* catch up on his romance.

*He took one look at the painting and all the air in the room disappeared...*

*The Earl of Huntington (Hunt) is a silent partner in a successful gambling hell run by his two brothers. A well-respected member of the ton, he moves about in Society as an unknown agent for the Crown on its most sensitive matters. Lady Diana is a long-time friend of Hunt's with the ability to embroil herself in difficult matters that require his assistance. Once again, she needs his help, but this situation could be a major scandal if discovered.*

*Against his better judgment, Hunt agrees to her scheme, but this time the circumstances cause him to see the woman he'd always considered just a friend in a different way. The passion and desire that sparks between them must be squelched since she would never do as his Countess... Scandal follows her every move.*

Want to read the rest of the story? Visit my website: http://calliehutton.com/book/a-scandalous-portrait/

Look for *An Inconvenient Arrangement*, book 3 in the Rose Room Rogue series.

*Dante Rose, along with his two brothers, splits his time between their very lucrative gaming hell and working undercover for the British Government on sensitive matters. He is also quite the rake, and as his father's by-blow, has no title, and therefore no need to ever marry and produce an heir. He loves the ladies and his life exactly the way it is.*

*Lady Lydia Smythe, daughter of Viscount Sterling has an unusual talent. She can read, write and speak seven languages. She is occasionally called upon by the Home Office to help in a case that requires her knowledge. As a bright, independent woman, she has no need of a man since she supports herself quite comfortably with her assignments from the Home Office, a job she dearly loves.*

*When Dante and Lydia are summoned to the Home Office and given an assignment that requires them to work together, sparks fly. Some of them good, some of them not so good. She abhors rakes, gambling, and just about everything Dante stands for. Dante balks at having to bring a woman into his investigation. But when the investigation turns dangerous, will he acknowledge his growing feelings for Lydia and protect her?*

Visit my website for more information:
http://calliehutton.com/book/an-inconvenient-arrangement/

You can find a list of all my books on my website:
http://calliehutton.com/books/

# ABOUT THE AUTHOR

**Receive a free book and stay up to date with new releases and sales!**
**http://calliehutton.com/newsletter/**

*USA Today* bestselling author, Callie Hutton, has penned more than 45 historical romance and cozy mystery books. She lives in Oklahoma with her very close and lively family, which includes her twin grandsons, affectionately known as "The Twinadoes."

Callie loves to hear from readers. Contact her directly at calliehutton11@gmail.com or find her online at www.calliehutton.com.

Connect with her on Facebook, Twitter, and Goodreads. Follow her on BookBub to receive notice of new releases, preorders, and special promotions.

"You will not want to miss *The Elusive Wife*." —My Book Addiction

"…it was a well written plot and the characters were likeable." —Night Owl Reviews

*A Run for Love*

"An exciting, heart-warming Western love story!" — *New York Times* bestselling author Georgina Gentry

"I loved this book!!! I read the BEST historical romance last night...It's called *A Run For Love*." —*New York Times* bestselling author Sharon Sala

"This is my first Callie Hutton story, but it certainly won't be my last." —The Romance Reviews

*An Angel in the Mail*

"…a warm fuzzy sensuous read. I didn't put it down until I was done." —Sizzling Hot Reviews

Visit www.calliehutton.com for more information.

Made in the USA
Las Vegas, NV
04 July 2021

25916905R00118